THE MAGIC COMPASS

THE MAGIC COMPASS

THE ADVENTURES OF MAGGIE PARKER™ BOOK ONE

MARTHA CARR

MICHAEL ANDERLE

LMBPN Publishing
PMB 196, 2540 South Maryland Pkwy
Las Vegas, NV 89109

First US edition, December 2019
Version 1.01, March 2020
eBook ISBN: 978-1-64202-612-2
Print ISBN: 978-1-64202-613-9

THANK YOU

To the Early Readers Team
Kathleen Fettig
Michael Robbins
Debi Sateren
James Caplan
Michael Baumann

Special shout out to Grace Snokes, Lynne Stiegler, Judah Raine, Kelly O'Donnell and Stephen Campbell for their general badassery behind the scenes to keep everything running so smoothly.

From Martha

To all those who love to read, and like a good puzzle inside
a good story
To Michael Anderle for his generosity
to all his fellow authors
To Louie and Jackie
And in memory of my big sister,
Dr. Diana Deane Carr
who first taught me about magic, Star Trek,
DC Comics and flaming cherries jubilee

From Michael

To Family, Friends and
Those Who Love
To Read.
May We All Enjoy Grace
To Live The Life We Are
Called.

CHAPTER ONE

There was a flash of sparkling gold light just outside the window, followed immediately by a loud crack of wood splintering and the sound of chickens squawking in the backyard.

"What the hell?" Maggie Parker stood suddenly upright, holding very still to try and catch any more sounds. Her knee banged against the tall, wooden dresser and she let out a short breath of air, choking back a grunt of pain. Nothing.

No, wait, there's one. A loud clang, like something was knocked to the cement floor of the garage out back.

She looked out the window, down in the direction of the small garage at the back of her yard. Someone darted past the window, followed by another streak of gold light. "Oh, come on..." She let the words out slowly, sucking in her bottom lip even as her reflexes took over. Four solid years as a robbery detective will do that to a body.

Maggie easily dove across her bed and landed on her feet, sliding open the drawer in the nightstand. She scooped up her nine-millimeter service weapon and ran for the stairs in one fluid motion. The toe of her running shoe caught on the cracked wooden tread, third from the bottom but she caught herself and leapt down the last few, already building up speed. "Really have to fix that someday," she mumbled as her hand took the corner, moving faster.

Out the back door she went, across the small patch of grass, turned yellow in what passed for winter in Austin, Texas, cold air filling her lungs. She jogged past the chicken coop, only the two white feathery Brahma raised their heads to look at her, squawking before going back to pecking at the ground. The eight other chickens were warmly nesting in the coop.

In a matter of moments, she was in the side door of the garage, quickly taking note of the jimmied lock. Her trained eye told her it was done by someone with some skill.

She raised her gun, placing herself by the door in the confined quarters. "Whoever you are, you're not going anywhere. Picked the wrong house, dude." The metal shelves jostled as a rubber mallet and pliers slid off and hit the hard concrete. She raised her gun, keeping her breathing even. "Let's not make this any more complicated. Do the right thing and come up with your hands raised over your head, fingers spread."

"Son of a centaur." It was a deep, rumbling voice, clearly frustrated. Sounded like he smoked way too many cigarettes. He was muttering something else, but Maggie couldn't make out the words.

A strong odor of damp earth hit her in the face as the

man came into the center of the room, his arms by his side. He was no more than five feet tall with only a rim of grey hair on his shiny bald head, and baggy blue pants covered in dirt, held up by striped suspenders over a green wool sweater. Maggie relaxed, just a little.

She arched an eyebrow, even as she looked to make sure he didn't have an accomplice. "Were you looking for a warm place to hang out? This isn't a shelter, but I can help you find a place."

The slight old man huffed in anger and balled his hands into fists. "That again! These are decent enough clothes." His words came out in a whistle through his jutting front teeth. He patted the pockets of his pants, releasing another wave of the mossy smell. "I'm not homeless, Peabrain."

Maggie cocked her head to the side, still holding up her gun. "Okay, name calling, very nice. Well, which one of us is about to get arrested, asshole?"

"Asshole is just a nickname. My friends call me Bernie." He spat the words out, his face flushed. "*You* can keep calling me asshole."

"Bernie, you're an odd combo for a criminal. You broke in here like you've done this before, but you've been banging around like you left your glasses somewhere."

He cut her off, waving his arms. "I have never needed glasses! Slipped on that grease stain." He looked back over his shoulder and back at her. "Place needs a good straightening up, if you ask me."

"No one is asking and from the looks of things, you caused most of the mess." Maggie lowered her gun, letting out a deep breath. "Look, Bernie, I'm gonna need an explanation." She waved her hand at the mess in the garage.

"Your training, I suppose," he muttered, taking a small step to his right.

Maggie furrowed her brow, tucking a long strand of brown hair behind an ear. "Do we know each other?" Her shoulders dropped down a little. "Oh geez, are you one of my mother's friends? Was she doing another white lady sweat lodge? Are you high on something?" She shook her head. "That collection of people she has in her house, no offense."

"None taken, I'm not one of them," he grumbled. He took another small step to the right, sliding an old green metal tool box with his foot. Half of the tools were already spilled out onto the floor.

Maggie looked at the toolbox and up at Bernie. That was the clang she had heard earlier.

"What the hell are you doing with Poppy's toolbox? You break in here to steal some old tools?" An ache centered in her chest. The tools were the only thing her grandfather had left her in his will last year. She had put the box on a shelf and left them there. It was still too painful to look through them. But it didn't mean someone could take them. "Answer the question. What do you want with the tools?"

Maggie lifted her gun back up, the hair on her arms starting to stand up and a familiar tingle spreading along the back of her neck. She got it every time something was about to go down. The muscles across her back tensed.

Bernie peered at her, squinting his eyes like he was sizing her up. He shrugged and turned, picking the metal box up and dumping out the contents.

"Hey! That's all I have left from my grandfather."

Maggie felt a flush of anger and ran across the room, dropping to one knee. She was still holding up her gun even as she pushed the tools out of the small man's reach. But he was already ignoring everything except the small wooden puzzle box that was resting lightly in the palm of his hand. A satisfied grin broke out across his face.

"Not a chance!" Maggie shouted.

He had picked Maggie's favorite from the tool box. A useless wooden box her grandfather let her play with as a child but was never able to open. It was decorated on every side with a different element of wind, fire, water or earth. On the top was an engraving of a compass rose. Bernie looked all around and waved his arm as he made an attempt at an end run around the detective, barreling at her. She put out her foot to trip him up, combining it with an elbow to his midsection.

"Oof!" He blew out sharply, losing his grip on the box as it dropped toward the floor. "No, not this time!" he called out.

They both reached up for the box at the same time, fumbling it through their fingers as it continued to tumble off course, headed for a puddle of water where rainwater had seeped inside the garage. The box landed on its side, making a small splash as Bernie gasped, his eyes growing wider. His voice came out in a whisper. "Peabrain, what have you done?"

"What?" Maggie looked back and forth quickly between Bernie and the box, which was already vibrating, the shaking growing more violent by the second. Maggie didn't hesitate.

She scooped it up, cradling it in her hands and felt the

vibrations from it travel up her arms, chattering her teeth. A wave of energy passed through her that felt exactly like the last time she rode a roller coaster and flipped upside down, twisting around a steep curve.

"How is this possible?" Her voice had a hum to it as if her entire chest were vibrating. But just as suddenly, it stopped, and the stillness hung in the air. She swallowed hard and realized she was still gripping her gun in her other hand. "Hope you don't have plans, Bernie because I'm going to be asking you questions for a while." Maggie never took her eyes off the box. A shudder went down her spine.

Bernie stood frozen right where he was, his mouth hanging open as one by one, different parts of the small box in Maggie's hand shifted and pieces unfolded like petals, revealing an inner chamber. Inside was a small brass compass with five black needles pointing in different directions covered with a clear glass face. One of the needles was pointing directly at Maggie.

"The compass, it was yours all along," gasped Bernie, staring at Maggie. "You're the new Elemental." The compass began to make a whirring noise, the needles spinning as the tiny cogs behind it spun, faster and faster. The round knob on the top of the compass popped open, pushing it up at an angle and small, metallic wings spread out to the sides, fluttering as the compass took flight.

Maggie watched the wings movement. "I'm pretty sure this is not possible," she whispered, as the intricate piece of machinery hovered in front of her face. She put her hand up closer to it and it dropped back into her palm, the wings folding up as the knob popped back into place. She heard

Bernie swear under his breath. "Leo swore it couldn't be you." Bernie put out his hand to touch the compass, laying inert in the center of the open box, still in Maggie's hand.

"Back off!" Maggie recovered herself, remembering why she was standing in her garage on her morning off. She kept out her hand that held the compass, not sure what to do but made sure her other hand was pointing her weapon at Bernie.

"You're going to need to put those hands up, Bernie. I haven't forgotten that you broke in here. You're coming downtown with me unless you can give me a *really good* reason for why you know the first thing about me and how that connects to breaking into my garage and what you want with Poppy's tools."

"Not the tools..." Bernie wiggled his fingers above his head, muttering the same garbled words Maggie had heard before but she still couldn't make out what he was saying.

"What are you..."

Large, clear bubbles floated in a cluster near the ceiling of the small, cinder block garage caught her attention. Maggie frowned but didn't have time to do anything more than that.

An old ball peen hammer rose off the floor from the pile of tools and landed neatly in Bernie's open hand.

Maggie felt another shudder go down her spine but there was no time to make sense out of any of it. "Have to stop eating brownies from Mom. I told her that wasn't cool after the last time."

Bernie's arm was already pulled back, launching the hammer in the direction of Maggie's head, leaning into the pitch. She ducked just as the hammer breezed past her head, tucking her chin, just for a moment. "Okay, now we're done playing. Attacking an officer guarantees you that ride downtown."

Maggie's head was only tilted down for a second but when she looked up Bernie was gone, and so was the compass. "Not a chance he got past me." She ran across the short divide, ducking behind the metal shelves but there was no sign of him. "How the hell did he get past me?"

A large moth fluttered near her head, and she swatted at it, her head still working on a swivel.

"Ow, did that thing just bite me?" She pulled in her hand and saw two small red marks. "I just got bitten by a baby mothra." She looked back up. "What a weird day." Out in the yard the chickens were all out of the coop, running along the fence squawking. Maggie ran to the fence, easily jumping up onto the wooden cross bar to get a better look into her neighbor's yard. No sign of Bernie anywhere.

She ran down the side of her Caribbean-blue bungalow and out to Pressler Street, but it was sleepy this time of day. A man in a green puffy coat with the hood pulled close against the wind, hurried along the street, not bothering to look back at Maggie. A small black Labrador looked up from a front yard two doors down and started barking at Maggie till she darted back the way she came. "Damn, where could that old man have gone?"

The chickens continued to race back and forth as the moth took to higher ground, flying closer to the top of the old pecan tree. It landed in the crook of the old tree where it was hidden from view, just as a large bubble *popped* next to it, releasing the small compass. The moth settled on top of it, biding its time.

Maggie's brow furrowed as she jumped down from the fence, looking for any further signs of trouble. A white and black Dorking hen nipped at the wire fencing surrounding the coop, clucking loudly. "Calm down Gertie. The trouble has already passed." She let out a sigh, one hand on her hip. "Best alarm system there is in my own backyard and that asshole got in and got out without a peep from anyone of you. Damn, what the hell just happened?"

She rubbed the marks on her wrist. "Did a compass really fly?"

CHAPTER TWO

M aggie's sister, Diana stood in front of her repeatedly snapping her fingers close to Maggie's face.

"Okay, slow down. You saw Poppy's tools fly? The puzzle box flew open... Crap, I told Mom no more potlucks with her friends. It's on you if you ate dinner over there. Can you tell me what's three times five?" Diana's wavy red hair was in a thick braid down her back, and she was wearing her favorite Wonder Woman t-shirt. The sisters looked just alike except for their hair.

Maggie pushed her sister's hand out of her face, laughing. "Not while you're doing that! Come on, Di, you're a doctor, aren't you? Does that sound do much for any of your patients?" They were sitting on Maggie's back porch, bundled up in sweaters.

Her sister smiled. "No, but I'm a bone surgeon and they're normally out cold and even when they're awake they don't *see* things." Diana tapped her head. "Different kind of doc."

Maggie got up and paced in front of her older sister. "I don't think this one is on Mom." She glanced at her sister. "Don't roll your eyes at me. Not unless Mom's group is baking something that causes momentary delusions that quickly fade."

Diana's face gave a hint of concern. "You're really worked up over this. Burglaries normally make you calm down." Maggie turned to pace the other way as Diana kept talking. "You work like a machine, like an AI." Diana pumped her fist in the air. "What? I admire it." Diana pulled a metal lawn chair closer, brushing off leaves from the tree before she sat down. "Entirely possible Mom's in this somewhere. Her friends are super clever. They're legit hippies who all came here to get their bones out of the cold weather and some of them have advanced degrees. I can see them coming up with some new hallucinogenic. It's like it's their frickin hobby."

"It wasn't Mom, and you're not helping. This was something else."

Diana leaned forward and let out a laugh. "Only other answer is that you saw inanimate objects fly. Come on, Maggie…"

"It's true, I swear." Maggie swore under her breath.

"You have Dad's mouth… but you swear like Mom."

"That one never gets old for you, does it? Come on, help me pick up Poppy's tools and save what's left of the box. Maybe it'll give me some clues."

"Maybe it'll start talking and just tell us what happened."

"Keep it up and I'm telling Mom."

Diana stood up, brushing off the back of her tight jeans.

"That'll be the day and we both know Mom has a limited capacity for listening. Besides, you never even told Mom it was me that talked you into rollerblading down West Lynn."

"West Lynn during rush hour." Maggie rubbed the faded scar just above her right eye. "I was old enough to make up my own mind. Besides, before I hit that speed bump it was one smooth ride."

"Speed bumps are dangerous. I've set more than one kid's bone because of those things. A hazard."

Maggie gave her sister a crooked smile. "Aren't first borns supposed to be the grounded ones?"

"Have you met our mother? I *am* the grounded one. Okay, compared to you, I practically have wings." Diana waved her arms in front of her body. "This is a big step up from where the family tree was headed."

"Not that we're judging…"

Diana let out a laugh. "Never. Mom's good people and she got us upright and employed, all on her own."

"Despite…" whispered Maggie as the smile slid off her face. The silence hung in the air for a moment.

"You have to forgive her someday, you know. None of that was easy. A freak accident killed Dad, not Mom and it was a long time ago."

"She still drinks, doesn't she?"

"Fair enough, give a balanced picture at all times." Diana gave her sister a small salute. "You know, we're all grown now. You can stand down."

"I like to think I pour all of those useful hovering skills into being a good detective." Maggie was doing her best not to let an edge come into her voice.

Diana tilted her head to the side, just like Maggie was doing. "Ever wonder what we'd be like if Dad had lived?"

That was enough for one day. Maggie didn't ever like thinking about losing her gentle father who liked to read and kept stacks of books near every chair in the house. She changed the subject. "Bernie had this weird earthy smell to him. Would have thought there'd be some good stank mixed in. Did I tell you about the bubbles? Big, large bubbles all bunched up together near the ceiling."

Diana let the conversation move on without an answer. It was what big sisters did. She sat back down and rested her cheek on her fist, watching Maggie put her hands on her hips and stand up straighter. It was the same tell she'd had since they were kids. She had a childhood knack for turning dark moments into something adventurous. There was no turning back now. "All seems unrelated to me. Not getting any connection," said Diana. "Didn't you say that old garage leaks? Maybe it's something to do with condensation."

"Never seen bubbles in there before and these were *big*." She held her hands a foot apart.

"Okay… massive fart bubbles, or old guy was making something before you found him, or hey, what about a sign from the cosmos? You were visited by aliens."

Maggie shook her head, her hands still on her hips. "First, ewww. No, this all fits together, I can feel it. Don't know how yet, but I'm gonna' figure it out and get that damn compass back."

"That's what makes you such a good detective. You love riddles, the weirder the better and can't walk away from a challenge." Diana stood up and hugged her sister. "Also what makes you a good sister. Go see Mom before you head to work and tell her your theories. She'll be so far out of the box with her answers that it just might spark an idea in you. I gotta go. Surgery awaits. Have to go put a hand back together again." She waggled her hands as she headed out the door. "Make sure you keep that second date tonight with what's his name. Bob, Christopher?"

"It's Jake, the fourth date and well, maybe."

"Oooh, fourth date, wear your good underwear. Aren't you glad you let me do all the swiping? I knew I could pick a winner." Diana started down the steps.

"So, we're going to forget about the guy who sold t-shirts out of his car and chewed with his mouth wide open. When are you going to get on a dating app?"

"No time, I'm always on call. Save the eye roll, I'm saving lives. What does he do, again?"

"Manages a CVS."

"Drugstore manager, okay. Stable, predictable, could be good."

"Nice, you hide your boredom so well. I'm going to figure this compass thing out." Maggie could still feel the remnants of the humming moving along her spine.

"I have no doubts," her sister called back over her shoulder, as she headed down the driveway.

CHAPTER THREE

Bernie brushed the dirt off the front of his jacket, stirring the air with a damp, earthy smell. The odor was always clinging to the old gnome.

He stepped off the curb at Lavaca near the corner of West 4th, still trying to take in that he had captured the compass and identified another elemental. "A Peabrain no less," he muttered. "I thought that part was a myth."

He heard the screech of tires before he saw the car hurtling toward him, but he was well over a thousand years old and had seen a little bit of everything through the ages. He quickly held up his arm as a streak of gold escaped his fingertips and a trail of large, translucent bubbles bobbed along, hurried by the gnome puffing out his cheeks and blowing them around the cars as they screeched to a halt inches from him. The surprised driver of a red Subaru laid on his horn as an afterthought before putting his hand to his face in shock.

A mother turned around to see if her kids were okay in

the back of her white minivan, yelling at them to stop arguing.

"Blast! Not a phone." Bernie spotted the phone in a pedestrian's hand, already recording the entire thing. He waved his hand again and more bright streaks of gold shot out, surrounding everyone in the area till they glowed in unison for just a moment. The light quickly faded as one by one, the bubbles popped snapping everyone back to reality. The Subaru driver smiled and turned up her radio, waving at Bernie as he finished crossing the street. The kids in the minivan settled back and looked around at the nearby shops, the argument forgotten as their mother let out a deep sigh.

Bernie snorted, satisfied at his handiwork and kept walking toward Republic Square Park and the necessary patch of wide-open green space.

He looked up in time to see a flash of gold and a familiar face heading back to the park. Another gnome.

Bernie grimaced. "Great! I'm definitely going to hear about this one. Car didn't even touch me this time. You get bruised in a smash up once and hear about it for a millennium." He quickly made his way down 4th street getting closer to the park, patting his shirt every few steps to make sure the precious compass was still with him. He felt the small metal object and took an easier breath that abruptly caught in his throat as he locked eyes with a man with silver hair, wearing a green puffy coat. "Simon..." gasped Bernie. The gnome thought he'd done a better job of hiding from the trackers.

Someone had spotted him and relayed the message to their leader, Simon Wesley.

Bernie grimaced, realizing things were getting worse. It wasn't like Simon to approach him in public like this. After all, he had secrets to hide too.

The gnome was still too far from the park to be able to escape. But there were too many people around to pull off any magic and still have time to make them forget. Not if he was going to fend off an attack at the same time. He pressed his hand to his shirt and picked up speed, even as Simon dodged traffic coming down 4th street, running toward Bernie. He caught the glint of light off the knife barely hidden in Simon's hand. *That must be meant for me. He's getting sloppy. He must know about the compass.* "This is bad."

Bernie knew the consequences if he was to battle Simon out in the open. Too many Peabrains would witness it. There was a chance one or two might wake up and convert. It was Rule Number Two, no assisting humans to remember they're magical. The punishment was imprisonment. "Like that could happen on this broken-down blue marble." He knew the governance committee would never hear about it from this far away. At least not till somebody could find all the parts to fix the machinery.

No one was going anywhere, and no information was getting out. Might as well stand his ground. The compass was too precious.

He turned just as Simon caught up to him and swung his right arm, slashing one of the gnome's suspenders and pricking his skin. Bernie winced but didn't back up as people on the street scattered, some screaming as they ran away. The gnome narrowed his eyes and wiggled his fingers sending a streak of gold pocked with sharp thorns.

The magical vine wrapped around Simon's arm and yanked him backward, but he was already whispering into existence a series of bubbles. They split into two groups, one streaking away. Bernie looked at the watch on his wrist. It wouldn't take the messenger bubbles long to alert others in Simon's group. The street would be overrun soon, and chaos would break out. He had to end this, and do it now, by any means necessary.

"No half measures!" he shouted, balling up his fist and landing a solid punch on Simon's jaw, momentarily dazing him. He didn't hesitate, lifting Simon over his head like a ragdoll and shaking him, even as Simon slashed through the open air.

Bernie let out a cry of pain as the tip of the knife cut along the back of his hand. A thin stream of dark red blood instantly appeared, and he felt a surge of anger as he tossed the man into the middle of the street.

Simon hit the ground hard, the wind knocked out of him and rolled to one side, struggling to stand. He wasn't done yet.

Bernie rubbed his large, thick hand against his jacket. "Bo-back-slappy-ass!" It was one of his favorite words he'd learned from the Peabrains. It could apply to almost any situation. He reached inside his coat, ready to pull out the sharp, small scythe.

"No, Bernie!" The gnome he had seen heading to the park was nearly by his side, running as fast as his stature would let him. He was still obeying Rule Number Two.

"Blast it, Jack! I have the compass, bend a rule once in a while. Use the bubbles!"

Jack covered the ground between them and pushed

Bernie behind him. "No, you're a Huldu. We don't break the rules!"

Bernie was flustered and said the first thing that came to mind. "I'm a gnome, you're a Huldu!"

"Potato, potato. We are the caretakers! Go on brother, bubble up behind me and get away. I'll hold off Simon and clean up this mess."

"Send someone to follow the Peabrain, the girl! She's an elemental," hissed Bernie.

Simon jerked his head around and looked at Bernie momentarily, his mouth hanging open.

"It's true, the compass came to life in her hands. We have to protect her before anyone else finds out."

"Go, I'll take care of it. Go!"

CHAPTER FOUR

M aggie jogged the short distance from her sister's house to her mother, Toni Parker two blocks down Pressler. None of the Parker women had moved very far apart.

Her mother's large three-story gray stucco home spread across two lots and had a porch offset by wide pillars. There was a broad array of lawn ornaments from a large silver gazing ball resting among ferns to two large metal cutouts of dragons standing over the winter pansies and faeries tucked under the azalea bushes. The collection had taken over most of the front yard. Her mother had perfected the art of decorating with tchotchkes.

The low thumping sound of steady drum beats was coming from the backyard and a familiar smell wafted toward Maggie as she took the broad, painted steps two at a time and went through the front door. It was never locked. Toni Parker had an open-door policy, despite Maggie's occasional protest. "That had better be patchouli," Maggie whispered as she shook her head and walked down the center hallway that ran the entire length of the house, and out the back door. She resisted the urge to look in the trash on the way through the kitchen and check for empties. *Not my business.*

Grackles came to rest on the tall street light on the edge of the property, letting out loud squawks as they settled their dark black feathered wings. Maggie barely registered the noise. They had been part of the background in Austin, Texas for as long as she could remember.

Bernie slipped down the street and glanced up at the birds as he made a perfect O with his mouth, blowing out a dark blue bubble that floated up to the birds and popped as it reached them.

The birds let out another loud chorus of screeches and took off, noisily taking flight. At the last moment, they split into three groups, heading off in different directions. Three of them flew to the large crepe myrtle in the backyard and landed neatly on branches near the gathering seated on lawn chairs.

The Huldu gnome watched until he was sure the birds were all safely on their way. "Want something done right, do it yourself." His hand had a thin wound along the back, still oozing a trace of blood.

He took another look around to make sure he was alone and released enough bubbles to cover his stout, little body as he shrunk down, turning into a large, yellow tabby cat. He hurried to the wooden fence, easily scrambling to the top of the gate and dropping into the backyard. Sharp barking warned the cat of an approaching menace.

"Oscar! Come here, boy." Toni yelled to the spotted pointer circling the cat, who hissed and arched his back as he quickly ran toward a circle of women sitting around different-sized drums. Toni pulled Oscar closer even as he let out a low growl, staring at the cat. "That's enough, this is a safe zone for all creatures."

Maggie crossed the large backyard, and came to stand by her mother, hands on her hips. "Mom, a safe zone for what? You're in a backyard in Central Austin. It's a very large safe zone."

"This must be your daughter!" An older woman with long silver hair piped up, smiling broadly at Toni. Maggie's forehead wrinkled as she looked at the woman, a newcomer to the backyard drumming circles that would spontaneously appear and sometimes last for days.

"You look just like your mother."

Maggie tensed, waiting for it.

"No, she doesn't. She looks like her father. Her sister favors me."

"Thanks Mom."

Toni tilted her head to one side, smiling up at her daughter. "It's a good thing. I see a piece of your dad every time I look at you."

She took a closer look around the yard. "Everyone looks a little too chill, Mom. We've talked about this…"

"Relax, it's just a little sage burning. I told you, we're on the straight and narrow since you busted us."

"Narrow-ish. Hi Maggie."

"Hi Mrs. Fletcher, nice to see you again."

"Larry still asks about you."

Maggie's mother smiled up at her, still holding onto Oscar. "Lucy, give my daughter a break. That was just a few dates and it was months ago. She's onto someone new, right? Sit down, Maggie, tell me what's up. You're doing that Wonder Woman pose. I sense something is afoot." Toni rubbed her hands together, delighted.

"Can I talk to you inside?" Maggie raised her eyebrows, not moving from where she stood, hoping her mother would relent. She already knew the answer and let out a resigned sigh.

"What's wrong with here? Half the people don't hear well anyway." Her mother snorted and waved her hand. "The others are deep into their drumming. Come on, sit down. Tell me what exciting thing has happened." Toni grabbed her hand and gave it a gentle tug as the cat let out a soft purr and stretched out on the grass.

"What started the drumming session this time?"

"Kathleen said there was a disturbance in the force. Have you met, yet? This is my daughter, Maggie Parker."

"I've heard a lot about you." The wrinkles lining Kathleen's face grew even deeper as she smiled.

"Kathleen's lived in the neighborhood for as long as anyone can remember."

"I'm an old timer." She held up her hand and held it steady in the cold air. "Felt the tremor earlier this morning. Energy just shot through the neighborhood."

Maggie felt that same familiar tingle across the back of her neck and a tightness in her chest. "What do you mean by energy?"

The cat let out a yowl and pulled away from the woman stroking its neck. "Oh, poor tabby, you're injured!" The others were distracted as Toni got up to go inside the house. The old woman leaned in and grasped Maggie's hand tightly, pulling her down into a crouch next to her as she whispered, "Everything is connected in this world, keep that in mind."

"Okay... not sure what to do with that."

"The birds, the trees, and everything in between, always talking to each other, sending messages." The woman let out a laugh, but the smile dropped from her face momentarily. "You were visited by a Huldu, am I right? A short little man with attitude?"

Maggie sat back on her heels as her eyes grew wide. She stared at the ordinary looking woman. "How do you... What do you..."

"Clever little creatures, really, even if they see themselves as the caretakers of the planet. I suppose they are, after a fashion."

"How do you know anything about this?"

"That's an easy answer that's quite complicated. I'm aware of the magic that's all around us. Happened to me years ago. They call it *waking up* when a human being remembers how to create using magic."

Maggie let out a frustrated breath and caught herself. If she could listen to what Kathleen was saying in between the crazy, maybe she could find out something useful to track the old man and the compass. "What's a who-who?"

"That's a whole *other* topic. I'm talking about a Huldu. A very ancient people, well, gnomes really. They live forever, well over a thousand years. Not sure I know how long they last beyond the stories I've heard."

Maggie was used to interrogations that didn't follow a straight line by people who dressed up the facts. This was going to be no different. "What did you call them, caretakers?"

"Yes, they make sure everything is running as it should from behind the scenes. A whole system of rules about the world and magic. Although their cousins, the Kashgar would probably point out that nothing is running correctly. I mean, after all here we all sit, not going anywhere."

"You're not making any sense. Can we get back to what's a Huldu?" She kept her voice low and steady, trying to keep Kathleen on track as if they were in a small room at the precinct.

"I believe I told you. It's a gnome, a magical being. The hired help, in a way." Maggie shook her head. "But that's obvious, and what's not magical? I mean, after all, everything is connected. Keep that in mind. It'll serve you well."

Toni came back with a salve for the cat's neck. Her thick auburn hair was piled on top of her head, held precariously in place by a silver clip.

She went over and scooped up the cat easily with one hand, pulling it close and sat back down in her chair. The cat settled into her lap, looking up at Maggie as Toni tended to its wound. "I can see you're confused."

"Not confused, just not high."

Toni arched an eyebrow even as she smiled at her daughter. "You need a boyfriend or at least get laid once in a while. Are you taking care of..."

"Mom!" Maggie cleared her throat, even as the drumming paused for a moment and felt her face getting warm. "Said that a little louder than I intended."

"Let me make this easier for my practical daughter." She smiled at Maggie, gently rubbing the cat's fur. "Kathleen is a sage, a keeper of old knowledge, right?" Kathleen smiled at Maggie's mother as the cat squirmed in her lap, trying to get away. "Not quite done, kitty. Hang in there." Toni looked up even as she applied the last dab of ointment.

The old sage studied Maggie's face as if she was looking for something. "Hmmm, I thought for sure something momentous had happened this morning. Maybe I was wrong. No awakening?"

"Nothing beyond realizing mixing Trix and Cocoa Puffs together was a genius breakfast move."

Toni let out a laugh. "See? Just like your Dad… and your Poppy, I might add. Marjorie, let me help you, honey. That's too much fat wood." Toni got up, the cat still held firmly in her arms and crossed the yard. The cat twisted around till it could look over Toni's shoulder, staring at Kathleen.

Kathleen watched Toni go, holding up a finger. "Wait just a moment." When Toni was further away, she turned back, pulling her purse into her lap

"Let me help you, just this once. It's breaking a Huldu rule, but who cares? I'm not a Huldu." Kathleen reached into the cloth purse and pulled out a clear ball that fit neatly into the middle of her palm. Inside of it was a small, perfectly formed tree. "Here, this is yours now." Kathleen didn't wait for a response and took the ball, pressing it into Maggie's hand.

Maggie held it up closer to examine the tree, marveling at the craftsmanship, just as a tiny black bird flew from the branches, circled the tree and disappeared back into its depths, rustling the leaves.

She startled and stared harder at the ball. "Was that a grackle?"

"Not to worry, none of that is real. It's like a Huldu picture, but we can create them out of what we know. I made this one to remind me of the Huldu's first rule. Rule number one is everything is connected, therefore everything is precious. Necessary tenet if you're transporting so many living things on this giant ship."

Maggie stared at the ball, trying to see how it was possible. "Is this a tiny computer? Look how small they can make them now."

Kathleen let out a sigh. "Nothing, huh? Okay, I tried. You're a tough case. Still, I would have sworn you'd crack open. Nothing strange happen at all today?"

Maggie hesitated but not for long. She needed information and there weren't many places to go ask someone about a flying compass and a little old man who disappeared into thin air.

"Someone broke into my garage this morning." She cleared her throat. "A little old man. He looked homeless to me."

"Another break in?" Toni had walked back over and stood next to her daughter, rubbing her shoulder. "What were they after?"

The cat yowled loudly and batted at Maggie's arm, its claws out. Maggie stayed just out of range and searched for the right words. "He was going through Poppy's old metal tool box and was about to steal that strange wooden box. You remember it, Mom? Had the different elements on it, one on each side."

"Another break in to that old garage. This is usually such a safe street," said Toni.

The smile had dropped from Kathleen's face and she sat

up straighter. "What happened to the box? Do you still have it?"

"I have the box, but not what was in it. The thing opened up, all on its own and there was a strange compass inside with five arms. The little man got all excited when one of the arms pointed at me, like it wasn't pointing north but straight at me."

"Then what happened…" The old woman said the words in measured tones, breathing harder.

"Then, uh, the damndest thing. The compass grew wings and flew for a moment before landing in my hand."

Toni looked at her daughter as the cat slipped from her hands and ran to sit a little closer to Maggie. "I knew there were a few of my special cookies missing."

"I thought you told me you were reformed."

"I am, there's no more smoking in the backyard. Bad for your lungs, anyway. How long ago did you eat one?"

"I haven't been in your stash, Mom, and let's go back to not wanting me to know anything."

Kathleen stood up and grabbed Maggie's hand again, squeezing it. "Where is the compass now?"

"The little guy took it."

"An old man got one over on you?"

"Thanks, Mom, and yes, he did despite me holding a gun. Strangest thing. One moment he was there and the next he was gone."

"That's not necessarily good news," said Kathleen, sharply taking in air. "You can't be sure it wasn't a Kashgar. That would put them one step closer to finding the others and the parts they need to fix the machine."

"That's a part to a machine?" Maggie's phone started ringing.

"No, it's a compass. Points you in the right direction. There's so much to tell you."

"Well, it'll have to wait. Work calls."

The cat slipped away from the crowd and out the way it had come, leaping over the fence. Moments later, bubbles rose into the air, popping as they floated away.

"It's your day off."

"Tell that to the bad guys. One of my old cases got a hit that can't wait."

"Take some coffee with you. It's still hot and you function better with a little caffeine."

"Mom, I'm heading into work. Not a good time for your idea of coffee."

"It's safe, I swear!"

"Well…" Mrs. Fletcher chimed in, "I put a few herbs in it. Mostly medicinal."

"Mostly… perfect. I'll stop at the Wag-A-Bag."

Maggie pulled away from the curb in the dark blue custom 1987 El Camino with a back seat and headed to the southeast side of Austin and the precinct near Slaughter Lane. She took a sip of the old coffee that had been sitting in her car since yesterday and choked it down. "Still coffee." She took another swig and swallowed hard. "Okay, just barely."

Her favorite convenience store was just across the river, over the South Congress bridge. She pulled into a space just in front of the only part of the large front window that wasn't covered by a sign advertising smokes or Clean Energy Drink. A neon sign blinked red and blue at the top, advertising chicken and waffles. *Made on site* was scrawled underneath in black permanent marker. She got out of the car, pouring the dregs of her coffee onto the blacktop, stepping up onto the concrete porch.

She pulled open the front door, a loud bing-bong announcing her entrance.

"Hey Joey, how's the coffee?"

Joey looked up from his sudoku puzzle, scratching his ear with the end of his pen. "Hot as always! One of my favorite people, now my day can really get going. Little late for breakfast, little early for lunch, but who cares. Take some chicken and waffles with you? The wife has been back there frying away, getting ready for the rush. We already sold out of all the breakfast taquitos."

"I think the word is getting out Joey. Locals have been talking up your cooking."

"Only way we can convince people to try our food. Otherwise who would pay to eat fried chicken out of the back of this old place? It's all Mamie and her recipes. Let me fix you a plate, put some homemade pickles in with it."

Joey was already walking to the back where there were two old metal tables set up, mostly for people waiting for their food. The operation was strictly carry out. Maggie made her way to the coffee pots lined up four deep by the chips rack and filled her travel mug to the edge, already trying to sip the hot coffee, swirling it around in her mouth. "Man, that's good stuff. Nectar of the Gods."

"Tastes even better if you don't burn your tongue." Joey smiled, shaking his head as he came walking up and handed over the heavy Styrofoam box. "Mamie had it ready, saw you pull up."

"My tongue can take it. I was raised on ghost peppers. Boy, that smells good." She slurped another gulp of coffee, as the loud bing-bong of the door chimed. She turned in time to see two men hustle their way into the convenience store, guns drawn. *Strange day.*

"How convenient. My work is now coming to me." Maggie carefully set down the box of food and her coffee and pushed Joey to the floor, behind the chip rack. "Stay down," she hissed, pulling out her gun.

"Drop your weapon, police!"

The burly man in front startled for just a moment but quickly recovered and turned, raising his gun in one fluid motion, pointing it at Maggie's mid-section. She saw the second robber pulling his gun and leaning to one side to get a clearer shot at her. *This is not going to go well.*

Maggie leaned to one side, getting off a clean shot and hitting the large man squarely in the chest, throwing him backward into his smaller accomplice, making his gun jerk up as he pulled the trigger. Joey pressed his palms against his ears, his eyes squeezed shut as he kept low in a crouch. Maggie heard a scream from the back of the store and resisted the urge to look back to make sure Mamie wasn't coming toward them. There was no time.

The second bullet was rapidly heading toward her and Maggie already knew it was heading toward its target. Right at her head.

CHAPTER FIVE

Time slowed down and she felt as if she could count the seconds, waiting for the very end of all things. "Dad," she whispered, an ache in her chest as she wondered if she was finally going to see him again.

Everything faded to black and she marveled that there hadn't been any pain, no sense of burning flesh, her head rocking back from the impact. *Who will take care of Mom and Diana?*

It was her last thought.

She felt the air rush out of her lungs, and she gasped for air, marveling that was still a necessity even when you're dead. There was a loud ringing in her ears and total darkness that quickly subsided, replaced by loud voices, arguing.

"Rule number nineteen! We don't interfere in life and death with the Peabrains! You broke a big one, Bernie. This is bad. This is very bad."

"I had to! Do you not understand this thing they insist is language? She's an Elemental with a capital E! The one who holds it all together. The main shebang!" Bernie's words came out in a whistle through his front teeth.

"That's no excuse. It'll throw everything off! She's now on borrowed time. Borrowed! She was supposed to be gone. That means there was no more story for her. Everything that happens after this is part of chaos." His voice was rising to the level of a squeak. "This never goes well. Events can change, Peabrains suddenly disappear and reappear…"

"Speaking of disappearing. We'll need to handle that mess in the Wag-A-Bag."

Maggie's vision slowly cleared. Through the haze she could see two short figures facing off, one of them waving his arms over his head and leaning forward as he yelled at the other. She squeezed her eyes shut, rubbing them and opened them again as the images became even clearer. So far, no sign of anyone she knew greeting her.

"Death is really not what I expected so far. Wait, is this… hell? Crap. Was it that time I told off the delivery guy for dinging my car? *That* was hell worthy? Come on!"

"Hey Jack, little ears are listening. We can pick this back up later."

"And we will. We have enough problems. It doesn't make it better that you brought an Elemental down here. That's a completely new system error."

Maggie felt the ringing go away completely and shook her head as her eyes came into complete focus. "Hey, wait a minute! I know you. You broke into my garage." Maggie slowly took in a deep breath and felt for her gun. It was still there. *Yeah, this is hell.* "Are you some kind of dark angel?"

"No, they live in Pasadena."

Jack elbowed Bernie and gave him a stern look. "Quit kidding around. Can't you see she thinks she's dead." He shook his head, tsking. "This always happens when a Peabrain slips through a crack into our operations."

"Literally." Bernie did his best to put on his version of a gracious smile. "Welcome to the inner workings of our world. Quite literally, again."

Maggie took in a sharp breath of air and felt her lungs fill. "Not dead," she muttered, stomping the ground with her foot, testing out the sturdiness of where she stood.

"Well, that's a new one, right Jack? Haven't seen one test out the ground underneath their feet before."

She took a look around in the darkness, peering into the distance but it was hard to make out anything. She rested her hand on her gun and took a step toward the two gnomes.

"Now, hang on sister. Don't even go for that gun," said Bernie. "Wouldn't even work down here."

"Down?" Maggie instinctively lifted her chin and looked above her head. She couldn't see a thing but could sense the ceiling was far above her. "Let me be clear. Not hell. Not dead."

"Not heaven either." Bernie formed a large transparent bubble in his hands and watched it zip out to Maggie, reforming itself around her gun as it disappeared altogether.

"Hey!" Maggie's hand slid down the side of her pants. "That's government issue."

"No worries, you'll get it back when you leave here. We have a few rules we actually follow." Jack glared at Bernie who shrugged. "No weapons, no cell phones. That last one is mostly to stop Leo from playing Barry Manilow on a continuous loop."

"He's a Fanilow."

"I was right the first time. This is hell." Maggie closed the distance between them, her arm out to the side, feeling for any kind of wall or structure. There was nothing.

"You can stop trying to figure things out. We'll help you, or Bernie will help you since he brought you here in the first place. Let's begin with a little light." Leo waved his arms as gold streaks shout of his fingertips, racing for different corners and lighting up the room with a warm, golden glow. Maggie's eyes widened as she saw the large cavernous room appear and long tunnels that stretched off in every direction, gnomes zipping by in the distance of each one. She looked down and saw tiles beneath her feet and above were hanging crystals. "Where are we?"

"Now, that is a question I can work with," said Bernie, tugging on his green sweater.

"Bernie, careful…" Jack gave him side eye, pressing his lips into a thin line.

"You're underground in the workings of the Earth."

Maggie knit her brows together, taking another step closer to the gnomes as Jack backed up a step. "I'm what?"

"Remember rule number fifty-two, Bernie."

"Rule, schmool." He leaned forward, emphasizing his words, which only made him whistle louder. "You're underground…" He spread his arms wide. "In the mechanical areas of the ship."

"What ship?"

"This ship."

Maggie looked around. "I don't see a ship."

"What do you mean you don't see it?" Bernie snapped his fingers in front of her face, lifting his hand over his head to reach her.

"For the love of… what is it with the snapping fingers? First my sister, now you." Maggie took in a sharp breath of air. "My sister… how the hell do I get out of here?"

"Easily done. You ready to go?" Jack hastily asked.

"Whoa, whoa, whoa," said Bernie, holding up his short arms and waving his oversized hands. "You can't give her the bum's rush. Were you not listening? She's an Elemental. The compass Elemental."

Maggie closed in on the gnome, towering over him as she leaned forward, their faces close together. "Where is my compass? You took it from me," she said in a slow, menacing tone. The events of the last few minutes were catching up with her and it wasn't sitting well with her that the gnome had stolen something from Poppy's tool box.

Bernie squinted one eye and arched an eyebrow over the other, making his face resemble a moon-pie Popeye. "You'll get it back when it's time and not a moment before. You have a lot to learn first." He scrunched up his face, staring back at her.

Maggie let out the breath she was holding. "Fine, start teaching me. Start with do I get to go back home?"

"Oh my, yes. No one wants you living down here." Bernie knit his fingers together, tucking his hands under his ample belly.

"No one wanted you to visit the mechanics, either." Jack crossed his arms, rocking back and forth on his heels.

Bernie put his hand on Maggie's arm and pulled her to the side. "Don't mind him. He's a stickler for the rules and oh boy, are there a lot of them. You'd think after thousands of years I'd have them all down, or he'd ease up a bit but neither one of those things has happened. Truth is…" Bernie sucked in air, letting out another whistle. "I'm not much of a rule follower."

Jack rolled his eyes and opened his mouth to say something.

"Zip it, cousin to a troll. I've got this." Bernie took Maggie's arm again. "You see, how shall I put this? Earth is a ship and at this point everything on it is cargo."

"Well, at least you eased her into it."

Maggie stared at Bernie's face, studying it for sarcasm or insanity. It was hard for her to point fingers about the crazy though, given her present circumstances. "You want to try that again?"

Bernie leaned in closer till with each whistle, a small stream of cool air and a little spit hit Maggie's cheek. "This…" Bernie waved his arms in a large circle over his head. "This is all an organic ship. Not that solid planet thing they teach you in elementary school. Kind of hollow. Hollow-ish. Modern technology from thousands of years ago. Uh huh, uh huh," he said in a hushed tone, nodding his head. "We are the mechanics of the ship, the guides."

"The crew," chimed Jack.

"Yes, yes, the crew." Bernie looked down at his feet for a moment but looked back up at Maggie, a resolute look on his face. "Rule number four. Rigorous honesty. Best and worst of the rules. Okay, you see, we had a little problem."

"Easy, Bernie." Jack took another step back.

Maggie looked pointedly at Jack. "Are there about to be explosions?"

"Well, a bombshell of sorts."

Bernie cleared his throat. "About twenty thousand years ago, we had to steer around a meteor shower…"

"You can *steer* the Earth. That's what you're saying." Maggie did her best to suppress a giggle. "I have gone crazy. Or is this the waiting room after you die? They test you here to see where to send you next. How do I pass so I get the good place?"

Bernie ignored her and went on with his story. "Not the first one to think that either." He snapped his fingers in front of her face. "Your sister's right. That does seem to work well with you. We had to steer around the shower, but we took the curve a little too sharply."

"You mean, you did."

"I was in charge that day, it's true. I was such a young gnome back then. We took that curve, got sucked into the stream of the Milky Way and whipped around, barely missing Venus and Mars till we wound up here. In the sun's orbit." He threw up his hands, still annoyed at the ancient memory.

"We've been stuck here ever since."

Maggie let out an annoyed sigh. "This is the best you have? A whacky story about Earth whipping around the solar system with a bad GPS? Who are you two, really? I'll bet I'm really passed out on drugs at the hospital."

Bernie pinched Maggie's arm, hard, and she slapped him.

"Whoa, whoa, whoa!" He held up his hands, leaning backward. "Just proving a point. You're not dead, you're not on a high somewhere, and you're not crazy," ticking them off on his thick, calloused fingers. "This has always been going on, but we hide it from most of our former passengers."

"You only have a few minutes to put her back in place, Bernie. Move it along with the story. Just cover the highlights."

"Fine." Bernie opened his mouth in the shape of a perfect 'O' and blew out a translucent blue bubble. The sweet smell of strawberries hung in the air, almost sickly sweet. He whispered words over it that Maggie couldn't understand as images appeared inside of it, creating different scenes. "Thousands of years ago, there were a few of these ships roaming different galaxies and acting as oversized ships to transport cargo and passengers. You Peabrains were passengers and would go from one place to another in giant herds. The Huldu gnomes, like Jack and myself, we are the mechanics who kept the ship running."

"The Kashgar, our cousins…" Jack rolled his eyes, shrugging.

"Those tall bastards, they live above ground with all the headroom. Of course, they grew taller!" Bernie calmed himself smoothing down the front of his sweater. "They were the muscle. They made sure nothing ate anything else topside. It was a great system that worked well."

Maggie listened trying to take it all in, watching the images appear in the bubble, fade and then another one appear. She reached out to touch the bubble, but Bernie gently held back her hand. "Stings like a mother if you touch someone else's bubble."

"Rule number fifty-four," said Jack, nodding. "Never mess with another man's bubble."

"But then we ended up here and all bets were off. A rift

started with the Kashgars somewhere around two thousand years ago."

"I was a much younger gnome, still had hair. This place was a regular paradise before that very bad day."

"Trouble really started with you Peabrains."

Maggie waved her hands in front of her face. "Wait a minute, what's with the Peabrain thing? Why do you keep calling us that?"

"It had a different meaning a long time ago."

Maggie was listening but suddenly felt a lurch in her gut and she let out a hiccup followed by a bubble that popped, letting out the sounds of Mamie and Joey screaming. "What the holy hell was that?" asked Maggie, even as she belched out another bubble.

"Can't hold this time gap much longer. We're running out of time, Bernie, speed it up. You took too long with the intro."

"Okay, highlights. Peabrain used to mean magical being. Humans were the most magical of all. It was a name of honor. You were a clever bunch." He was spitting out the words as fast as he could, feeling the pressure of time. "You even constructed this amazing library in Alexandria, Egypt that contained all the records of *everything* that had ever been known, anywhere."

"And he means anywhere. Covered all the Earth ships, all the different galaxies, all the destinations, everywhere. But you're not explaining the Peabrain part! Let me try. Humans have two brains." He held up two fingers. "That's right, two. The main brain we all know and love and a smaller brain buried at the top of your spine, along the back of your neck. Much smaller…"

"And so far, not detectable by science, thank you very much."

Jack rolled his eyes. "Bernie's the one who's been able to foil that a few times. Very proud of himself. And you're stepping on my explanation."

Bernie ignored him and plowed ahead. "That little brain…"

"The size of a pea…"

"Is the part that contains the magic. It's small in size…"

"And amazingly powerful! Blows the mind." Jack blew air out, expanding his cheeks while shaking his hands near his head.

"Peabrains, I get it," said Maggie. Pressing her palm against her stomach.

"It's why the hair on the back of your kind's neck tingles when you sense something exciting or dangerous. That little pea is stirring, but usually not enough to turn on the magic."

"Turn it on?" Maggie rubbed the soft, smooth skin along the back of her neck.

"Save something for later." Jack batted at Bernie. "There's too much to tell and that part… that should wait till we have to tell her."

Maggie wanted to interrupt but Bernie was already chattering away, deep into the story, talking loudly. The sound echoed off the machinery that snaked along the walls and down the different tunnels.

"The height of your magical abilities was the Library of Alexandria, at least so far. Took a special counsel of Peabrains coming together to pool their magic to do it, too.

It was an amazing feat. But, that's what helped the Peabrains find out they had been betrayed."

"By the Kashgar, tall dirty bastards!" Jack pounded his fist into the palm of his hand.

"We found out the Kashgar on *this* ship had made a deal to turn over everyone on the planet and put your kind into magical servitude, then chop shop the ship."

"You mean cut up the Earth?" asked Maggie, watching the images inside the bubble of the Library at Alexandria and its different gardens, and zoo and shrines. But just as quickly, the image started to blacken around the edges and catch fire inside the bubble, destroying everything.

"To gain immense power. The Kashgar wanted to cut off communication outside of this ship with other planets and burned the library and all its contents to the ground. They rounded up the most powerful Peabrains and sacrificed them to the lions," said Jack.

"They went old school on their ass. Turns out they had different plans. Someone had made them an offer and they wanted to seize the ship and take it to a different destination. Almost worked, too."

"Instead, the Huldus were able to take apart key pieces of the machinery and infuse them with magic."

"To hide them, we breathed each one into different magical creatures."

"We never thought it would take long to get moving again."

Bernie slapped his palm against his forehead and shook his head. "Boy, brother, you said it. Thousands of years! Still stuck right here!"

"One of them must have been an ancestor of yours,

which means you hold a piece inside of you."

"Who knew? You're the Elemental Human Peabrain."

"I'm magic," whispered Maggie in awe, pressing both of her hands to her stomach. A surge of air erupted from deep inside her belly and she covered her mouth, trying to hold it back. But it only made her belch louder, spitting out a continuous stream of bubbles as she felt a stronger lurch in her belly, jerking her backward. "What's happening?"

"That's the alarm. Time's up!" yelled Jack. "You have to go back, and on borrowed time!"

"But all I'm left with are questions! What do you mean borrowed? Do I have to give it back at some point?" Maggie felt the pull again and stepped back, almost falling over, the bubbles streaming out of her mouth in a continuous flow and the sounds of the Wag-A-Bag pouring out of the bubbles. "My gun!"

"Right! Right!" Jack opened his hand and a gold bubble emerged, zipping over to Maggie's side, popping to reveal her gun.

"Not to worry," said Bernie. "We'll be in touch. We even took care of that problem you're having with a bullet aimed at your head. Okay, I took care of it. I broke a rule, happy Jack?" Bernie harrumphed. He shook his hands in the air, making his case. "You're an Elemental and we need you to get this ship moving again. Watch out for the Kashgar, though. They want your kind dead. You most of all, you're the key to *everything*."

Bernie leaned forward, the round knob of the compass barely poking out of his pants pocket, pleading with Maggie. She saw it, at the same time she hiccuped loudly, and lunged for the compass, catching Bernie off guard. She clutched it in her hand as something yanked her back into darkness and Bernie yelled for her to stop. "There's so much you don't know! It's dangerous for you to have it. You don't understand."

"Tell the grackles!" yelled Jack. "They'll have to guard her."

"It won't be enough."

"Then it will have to be you!"

"What?" He let out a tinny whistle of air between his teeth.

"She's gonna need a guide."

Their voices grew fainter until Maggie found herself standing back in the Wag-A-Bag at the precise moment when she had left. She heard the second burglar's gun click as he fired and she braced herself, her hand squeezed around the compass. Just in time, she realized she had come back just six inches to the right. *Bernie took care of it.*

The bullet whizzed by her ear, a high-pitched whine breaking through the air. Instinct kicked in and she pulled out her gun, shooting the man as he fell backward onto the floor. A small pool of blood quickly oozed around his ribs.

"Alabar los cielos! Is it over?" Joey was still crouching on the floor, lifting his head slowly to look past the rack of chips.

Maggie's phone buzzed in her pocket and she pulled it out, her hand shaking. It was a text from Jake. *Looking forward to seeing you Saturday.*

"That's hard to say," said Maggie, still clenching the compass in her other hand. "It seems it's all just getting started." A small bubble floated out of her mouth, popping as it rose in the air.

CHAPTER SIX

The coroner took his time assessing the scene at the Wag-A-Bag, finally gathering up the two dead thieves. Outside, the grackles gathered across the phone lines screeching in unison as some took flight, only to be replaced by other large black grackles crowding the space. Joey sat in a chair behind the counter being comforted by Mamie, refusing the EMT's repeated suggestion to get checked out at the hospital.

"I have customers," he kept saying. "They will need their lunch."

"Dude…" said the young paramedic, "You're going to be closed for the day. It's gonna take a while to clean up this mess." He scanned the pools of blood already turning a darker color and shook his head.

Joey clutched his chest and looked up at Mamie, panic in his eyes.

"Joey, why don't we feed these nice people, instead. A little act of kindness in the middle of all this," said Mamie, gently.

The idea came over Joey and he took in his first deep breath in hours, the color seeping back into his face. "Yes, yes, what a good idea." He kissed Mamie's hand and took another deep breath, standing up slowly. The sadness came back over his face as he looked at the blood on the floor and the yellow tape, but Mamie gently tugged at his hand, pulling him away.

"This must be a hard job to do, mi querido. Don't you think? Let's go see how we can help."

Maggie stepped aside, mouthing, *thank you* to Mamie and marveling at how well the couple worked together. *Not my skill set at all.*

Two homicide detectives came in the door, making a beeline for Maggie.

"Kind of funny, you know. A robbery detective getting held up, right?" The tall, dark haired detective let out a snort and pulled out his iPad, making notes.

Maggie pressed her lips together, forcing a smile at Detective Easton. The jokes were beginning already.

"Too soon?"

"You mean five minutes later, Easton? No, not at all. I mean, you want to be first with the jokes, right?"

"Alright, I get it. My wife tells me the same things, daily. So, can you give me the basics and we'll get to the mountain of paperwork later?"

"I was in here to get coffee, like I do every day and two armed gunmen came in, weapons drawn. I announced myself as police and drew my weapon and defended myself. I shot before the first perpetrator could get off a shot and returned fire with the second."

Detective Easton scratched his head, looking around at

the distance between the row of coffee pots and the front door. "Lucky thing these two mooks were such bad shots. I mean, come on, both of them missing you. What are the odds?" He looked back down at the iPad and typed with two fingers.

Maggie pressed her hand against the compass in her pocket. "Pretty high, I imagine." She kept her voice calm and even, slipping into detective mode. "Sometimes you get lucky."

"Right, I suppose so."

Maggie walked into the precinct carrying two Styrofoam boxes of chicken and waffles, walking as fast as she could down the hall toward the large open room and her desk. She reached over and set one box down on her partner, Detective Peter Taylor's desk that sat opposite hers and pulled her chair closer.

"You trying to drum up your own cases these days, Parker? Austin a little too calm to suit you?" Detective Moss, an old veteran ambled over from his nearby perch on the edge of his desk.

Maggie gave the detective a crooked smile. She knew it was his way of asking her if she was alright. "Bullet missed me, so it's a good day and I got chicken and waffles thrown in for my trouble."

"That is a particularly good day." He opened the box, turning it around at different angles.

"You want a piece, Detective?" Maggie arched an

eyebrow, sliding it closer to him. "Help yourself. Not much of an appetite today, anyway."

The detective took out a leg and breathed in the aroma, smiling. "That your first shoot, right? That can be tough. I've been around here for over thirty years and only had to shoot once. Don't tell anybody but I missed the guy. Fortunately, he missed me too."

Maggie smiled, feeling her muscles across her back relax. She didn't believe the story, Moss was known for his high scores at the shooting range, but she appreciated it. The old robbery detective was never going to hold her hand and she didn't want that, anyway. Feelings were not her specialty.

Detective Peter Taylor came bustling in, dropping his brown lunch bag on his desk, his tie yanked to one side and his thick mane of grey hair standing up in places. He wasn't much younger than Moss. "You doing okay? I heard the basics on the scanner." He noticed the white box on his desk and breathed in deeply, eyeing his crumpled lunch bag and gave it a quick push into his grey metal trash can with a swipe of his large hand. "No one tell the missus. Claire would not be amused," he said, patting his belly. "She has me eating grass and avocado, damn rabbit food," he grumbled.

"Has she figured out you've been sliding Doritos in the middle?" Moss laughed and grabbed a second piece of chicken. "May I?" Maggie nodded, smiling. He took a bite without waiting for the answer.

"No, and we're gonna keep it that way. *This* is real food. From the crime scene? Good thinking, multi-tasking. I'll take it." He sat down at his desk and opened the box in front of him, closing his eyes and smiling. He shut it again and slid it to the side, narrowing his gaze at Maggie. "I hear that wasn't the only point of interest in your day? Something about another break in at your house." He held up his hands in protest, shaking his head. "Save it, I know you didn't file a report. This is still a small town for us locals. Your first mistake, you told your mother in front of her crew. They told a few others. Took about thirty minutes to reach me. Slow day for them."

"Not for you," mumbled Moss, looking up at Maggie, his mouth full of chicken. "And the day's not even half over yet. Trouble tends to run in three's. Just saying."

Maggie ignored him. "It was nothing. I got into a scuffle wrestling with a bald version of Gimli."

"Love Lord of the Rings. Claire and I are saving up for another trip to New Zealand. He get away with anything?"

"In the end, no. He was harmless."

Taylor shot her a look. He heard the catch in her voice but knew that determined scowl. "Given how the rest of your day worked out, I suppose that we can take a pass on your garage."

Maggie's phone buzzed and she looked down and saw Jake's number pop up. "I have to take this," she said, rising and walking away from the clusters of other detectives. Maggie was having a hard enough time trying to figure out dating.

"Hello?"

"Hey, how's your day going?"

Maggie didn't hesitate. She wasn't ready to tell him about her mother and her parties, much less falling through the Earth and narrowly avoiding missing a bullet meant for the center of her head. "Fairly routine. What's up?" She winced, realizing she sounded like she was trying to blow him off, but only because she was, and only because she didn't know what else to say. Ask about stolen items, or the way someone broke in, or how to get them to release hostages. Chit chat did not come naturally.

"Uh… did I catch you at a bad time?" His deep voice sounded caring, making it harder on her.

What am I supposed to say here? Can I phone a friend? "No, I was working a burglary at a convenience store. My mind is still there." *Not a lie.* "Looking forward to this weekend," she said, looking at the ceiling for inspiration. *I wish I could be somewhere else.*

She felt her pocket warm against her skin, almost burning and a light seeping out the edges. "What the hell?"

"What? What's happened?"

He does do a good caring-about-you voice. "Uh, something's come up here. Gotta go. Text me later." She hung up the phone as she heard Jake say, "Text me later."

There was no time to worry about the sound in his voice or what to say next. The palms of her hands were warming, and she felt that same hum down her spine as the ground beneath her feet began to vibrate. "No, no, no, no…" she whispered, looking around to see if anyone had noticed. No one was looking in her direction. "Not this again." She balled her hands up into fists and planted her feet, hoping to stop whatever was coming next. A bubble formed out of her mouth and she quickly swatted at it, breaking it apart even as an image of the park near her house was forming inside of it. The place her dad used to take her to play when she was small. It was the same image she held in her mind whenever she needed to relax.

A feeling of calm swept through her and the vibration settled down, the heat emanating from her palms and the compass in her pocket ebbed. Her breathing slowed and she made herself take in one deep breath after another and let them go.

"Must have been some hot phone call." Moss ambled past her on his way to the Captain's office, waggling his furry eyebrows at her.

"Yeah, the phone call." Maggie did her best to laugh at the joke.

"Hey Parker!" Taylor was waving the handle of his phone in the air. "Forensics called. They want to see you. Apparently, your mother has a deeper reach than I realized. Impressive."

Maggie took a few cautious steps toward her desk, still prepared to fall through the old vinyl blue and white tiles.

Taylor lowered his voice. "It's a good thing, kid. Your mom's looking out for you. You never know. That old guy might be trouble."

"Right, sure. How do you know my mother called him?"

"What else could it be? You didn't fill out a report. Go on, see what he wants. He sounded anxious." Taylor brought her a fresh cup of coffee in a cracked but clean mug that read, *10-4, Coffee That.* "I made it with two coffee packets the way you like it. Fresh but runs like mud."

"You do know me."

"About as well as you let anybody."

Maggie ignored the dig and slurped some of the hot coffee. *I have my reasons and they just keep piling up.*

CHAPTER SEVEN

Maggie rapped on the door and waited for Simon to look up from the evidence drying cabinet. "Hi Simon, you called?"

"Yes, Detective Parker, nice to see you." Even though Simon was in his early thirties his hair had turned completely silver years ago. He brushed his long bangs out of his eyes and stood up straighter, sliding his glasses back up his nose. "I wanted to offer my assistance."

"Did my mother... never mind. What kind of assistance?"

Maggie had never paid much attention to the specialist. He preferred staying in his lab and sending his assistants with the reports to talk to the detectives or beat cops. "I understand you had a break in, and the burglar got away with some of your valuables?"

Maggie stayed quiet. One of her own rules. Let someone talk themselves out. She tilted her head and waited, her hands on her hips.

"I know you don't want to file a report."

"Whoever has been talking to you was thorough."

Simon looked embarrassed and his face reddened as he looked down at his shoes for a moment. "This place is one large high school at the end of the day. Everyone likes to talk about what everyone else is doing. I couldn't even tell you who was the original source."

Maggie held up her hands. "It's okay, but I don't think there's anything to gather. Not much was taken, anyway. Just something that was sentimental and belonged to my grandfather." Another hard and fast rule of hers. Rigorous honesty at all times. It kept her out of a lot of trouble over the years, but it didn't mean she had to say everything.

"That's sometimes the hardest kind of loss. I don't mind. You've always been nice to me." He shrugged, tapping his fingers on the tan metal cabinet. Before she could say anything else, he blurted out, "It will give me a chance to go out in the field and use some of the new equipment." He gave a nervous smile, clapping his hands together. "And without the pressure of time. No detective waiting for a report so they can get on with an investigation. What do you say? I have some new fingerprinting equipment that's pretty advanced. Can take a print off almost any surface, even a partial. Might help you out if the guy is in the system."

A Huldu in the system. I suppose that's possible. Maggie bit her lower lip and thought about it a moment, her hands back on her hips. The adventure was starting. "I get the report right away?"

"Absolutely," he said, vigorously shaking his head. "Just you and it should even be by the end of today!" A smile spread across his face.

"But not on government time. It can't take you away from what you're doing for any cases." She gave him a small smile back. *He really likes his job.*

"Of course, my shift is up in a couple more hours. I'll be in and out of there in no time. Is the garage unlocked?"

"Uh, no, but there's a key under the potted rosemary near the door. Ignore the loud chickens, and lock up on your way out, please."

He nodded his head again, sliding his glasses back up his nose as his bangs slid down in front of his eyes. He pushed them back up and smiled. "You've always been nice to me."

"You're a colleague," said Maggie over her shoulder as she walked to the door of his lab, turning back for a moment. "You do a good job."

She passed by the closet, the door slightly ajar and inside a green puffy coat hung on a hook. Something nagged at her as she left but she couldn't quite put it together. "Not sure *I* even like the job that much," she muttered on her way to the elevator.

Simon saw Maggie glance toward the closet and clenched his fists, quickly opening his hands in case she turned back. To his relief she had kept walking and he made himself slowly go over and press the door shut. He left the coat at work and grabbed an older blue jacket with a busted zipper out of his trunk before getting in his car. He barely felt the cold wind, so relieved to have an excuse to take his time in Maggie Parker's garage.

It was his ground zero that he had been waiting for, for years.

He got to the address on Pressler Street and parked his car in front. No need to worry about anyone spotting him and asking what he was doing. He made his way down the side of the blue bungalow and through the gate carrying his oversized forensic toolkit, staring at his destination. The simple, small wooden structure in the back that could finally help him get the answers he needed. "Find the compass, save the world," he whispered. The chickens sent up a chorus of squawking, most of them retreating to the coop to get away from the stranger moving quickly through the backyard. He didn't even notice.

Simon's normally steady hand even shook as he tilted the rosemary plant, breathing in the sweet aroma. He scooped up the key and nervously chewed his bottom lip, unlocking the door and slowly pushing it open with a loud squeak.

He stood on the threshold slowly drawing in a deep breath and letting it out in a rush, feeling a sense of relief. "Here we go." He set the toolkit down just inside and gently shut the door behind him. It was mostly a prop to satisfy any nosy neighbors, except for the small tool nestled in a felt cloth underneath the top tray.

Simon took it out carefully and held onto it, hoping even still that there was a chance the compass was hidden nearby.

It was a brassy gold color and made of metal in the shape of a wishbone with an ancient language inscribed down each long piece that translated to, *what was lost can be found.*

It was vibrating just a little in his hands, reacting to the remaining traces the compass had left behind. Even that would fade in time.

"I was so close. One day late. Damn the Huldus. They'll get us all killed." He pushed his glasses back up his nose. "Guess it will have to be Plan B." His voice squeaked, his nerves showing. He pulled out a slip of paper from his pocket and mumbled the ancient words on it, practicing. He couldn't be sure what would happen if he got it wrong and he didn't want to find out. Not when he was this close. "Find the compass, save the world." It had become his mantra. He slid his glasses back up his nose and took one last look around the garage.

He held his arms out to his sides and shut his eyes, breathing in deeply. "Et fac connexionem in sanguinem, ligabis ad quod quarere. Et fac ita."

The hair across the back of his neck stood up, tingling. He let out the air as a large, translucent bubble appeared that quickly turned a deep red. He was making a blood bubble, dark ancient magic. It required drawing from his own essence.

He opened his eyes and admired the size and color of the bubble. It was his first attempt at using the blood spells.

The blood bubble hung in the air, slowly starting to spin, end over end as the color deepened, and the air took on a metallic taste. The smell of lavender permeated the room quickly taken over by the smell of rotten eggs. An image emerged of the compass safely tucked in a pocket.

The back of Simon's neck ached, and he felt as if his bones could splinter but he gnashed his teeth and held on, his arms still outstretched. His chest was heaving up and down from the effort and sweat appeared across his forehead, fogging his glasses. The blood bubble spun faster and faster, closer to his face till it popped, the droplets covering his face, quickly absorbing into his skin. His eyes darkened a deep red for a moment and he finally saw who held the compass.

"Noooooo," he hissed, realizing his mistake. "She had it all along!" His arms throbbed as they dropped to his sides. His heart was pounding as if he had been drinking coffee for days. He reached down for his glasses, his hand shaking and knocked them to the floor. He made himself take a few deep breaths, but his heart was still racing, and he noticed there was a mild ringing in his ears. He tried again, scooping the glasses off the cement and sliding them onto his face. "This can still be rectified, of course it can." He clenched and unclenched his fists. "But not by me."

Everything was carefully replaced in the kit, and he took out the tools needed to take fingerprints. Maggie would still be expecting a report. But before he started, he pulled out his phone and sent out a text. 'I'm going to need your help Meet me at Zilker Park by the sand volleyball courts in an hour.'

The response was almost immediate. 'On my way.'

Simon slid the phone into his pocket and quickly got to work. Maybe there was even still more to learn from a garage that had once held the magic compass for so long.

CHAPTER EIGHT

The day had moved quickly. Two burglary calls started off the afternoon with the accompanying amount of forms to fill out. Lunch was a hastily downed What-A-Burger that was sitting heavily in Maggie's stomach. "Next time we go to Hecho en Mexico." She patted her belly. Maggie and Taylor were pulling up to their third call of the day.

"Portions aren't the right size for a growing boy."

"I'm pretty sure you're growing in the wrong direction, Taylor."

Maggie got out of the blue El Camino and leaned back inside, her arm on the roof. She felt the compass sway in her pocket. She still wasn't sure what to do with it and leaving it behind in her desk or the glove compartment seemed like the wrong move. "Come on, check the scores later. You aren't actually throwing the football."

"Did you see that the Cowboys are thinking about Randall Cobb? Good choice for wide receiver."

"I don't understand the words that are coming out of your mouth."

Detective Taylor gave a grunt and slid his phone into an inside pocket of his jacket and grimaced as he got out of the car. He walked around, onto the sidewalk in front of the Austin Rock and Roll Car Museum that was tucked in a commercial section on the southeast side of the city. The building was a nondescript, one story white stone building with darkened windows. Nothing looked disturbed and there was almost no traffic on the street. The detective gave a glance down Commercial Drive in both directions, narrowing his eyes.

Maggie knew that look. "How much did you bet?" Maggie gave him a crooked smile. "Not the whole month's budget?"

Taylor looked around at the nearby office buildings. "No, I learned my lesson on that soccer game last year. That was a long month. I have a system these days. No more than a quarter of my fun money on any one bet. Still, losing hard earned dollars always has a little sting. But enough of my hobbies..."

Maggie let out a laugh. "You're still ahead of me. I need to get a hobby."

"What about your chickens?"

"They're more of an inheritance and come with a lot of work. I need a hobby that's just for fun."

"Like dating." Taylor gave Maggie a sidelong glance.

Maggie instinctively tapped the top of her gun, getting a snort of laughter out of her partner.

"Does this Jake guy know what he's dealing with?"

"Are you figuring out the odds?"

Taylor waved to the curator who was holding open the front door and waited for Maggie as they both crossed the broad sidewalk. "I find it's better to never bet against your partner. Hello, sir..." Taylor flashed his badge for the thin, neatly dressed man with a substantial black beard that was neatly trimmed and puffed out on all sides. "My name is Detective Taylor, and this is my partner, Detective Parker. I understand you've had a robbery?"

The man held his hands together to form a steeple with his fingertips, pressing them against his puckered mouth as he let the detective go by him, into the museum. Maggie smelled the sweet tobacco that had to come from a pipe on his clothes as she passed him. It reminded her of her father.

The man followed them in, swinging his arms behind his back, grasping his hands together. "I'm Frank Winters, the curator for the museum. I'm afraid we've had one of our rarer items stolen. A 1938 guitar owned by Hank Williams, Sr."

"I thought this was a car museum. Will you look at that? The Ghostbusters hearse. If that isn't nicer than a one-ton Longhorn." Taylor ran his hand along the back red fin of the white hearse, letting out a low deep whistle as the curator nervously followed him, sputtering syllables.

"It's mostly a car museum with a rock and roll flair." The curator let out a ragged cough.

Maggie let Taylor have his moment but got on with things. "I understand you told the officer that someone broke into the building. Nothing looks out of place. How can you be sure it wasn't an inside job? You have cameras and an alarm system, right?"

"We do, both bypassed and according to our security

people that should be impossible." Winters puckered his mouth again; a sour look on his face to match.

Maggie nodded, "Then what's leading you to believe it was someone on the outside?"

"Follow me." He walked briskly toward a back right corner of the wide open warehouse, as Taylor and Maggie followed. Taylor let out another whistle as they passed a black Mustang, but Maggie knew her partner was also busy taking in small details. Very little got by him even if he looked constantly distracted. It was part of his charm and made most people talk too much.

"I did not know this place was here," said Taylor, his chin up, looking at the ceiling as he did a quick turn, even as he followed Winters. Maggie saw the orange El Camino and brushed her hands across the chrome on the front of the shiny hood, earning a raised eyebrow from the curator. She gave him a thin smile and lifted her hand. "Something about an El Camino," she said. "Practical, unique and still beautiful."

"Indeed," said Winters, as they crossed the rest of the distance past a large car with an oversized dashboard full of buttons and several brass horns attached at the top. "Leave it!" He pointed a finger in the air, anticipating Taylor's next move.

Taylor let out a sigh and a shrug. He walked past a tricked out red Model-T. "Now, this is a great hobby."

"Still too much work." Maggie followed Winters down the back wall till they got to a back door.

"I almost missed it. Your forensic people tried to get a fingerprint, but they didn't look very happy." He pointed to a gummy residue left around the lock.

"Simon." The two detectives spoke at once.

"No worries, he always looks like that. It's his resting work face."

Winters folded his arms in front of his chest. "That explains a lot. Wouldn't answer a single question. He pulled some out of the lock too. Looked like someone was making an impression with some kind of rubber material."

"Why on the inside?" Maggie said quietly. She leaned down and looked closer. There was a tingle across the back of her neck, but she ignored it. That always happened when she was close to an interesting clue. *Not everything is about a so-called pea.*

Frank opened the door and pointed to the right by a neatly kept brick patio. "There's a footprint out back. Seems like a blunder for someone who got past sophisticated security measures." He held up his hand, shaking his head. "Not one of my people. We sweep the back every night. Whoever left that came in after we were all gone."

"Not much to go on. Can we get a look at your security footage?"

"Of course, the monitors are in my office. Follow me." He took a step but spun back around, doing a tight pirouette on his heel. "But no touching." He fixed a steely glare at Taylor who held up his hands.

The office was a small space only big enough to hold a desk and a few chairs, and the monitors against the wall made the space even tighter. Maggie waited for Winters to show the footage from the last night but had to slide past Winters to get closer to the monitor. The back of her neck tingled, sending a shiver down her spine, and she could feel her pocket holding the compass warming up. She glanced up at Winters' face, her hands on her hips and took in every detail about him. *Something is off.*

The smell of tobacco was even stronger with him standing so close to her. *Vanilla and bourbon.* That had been one of her father's favorite blends too. Still, it was only making her trust him less.

Winters had taken a position behind Maggie, pushing Taylor almost to the wall near the farthest monitor where he squeezed into a chair. Maggie saw a small tattoo of four small stars in a random pattern on the inside of his wrist poking out of his sleeve. Winters noticed and pulled his sleeve down, covering the tattoo. She tilted her head, narrowing her gaze.

He spread his feet, taking a stronger stance and crossed his arms over his chest, muttering something.

"What was that?" Maggie couldn't make it out.

"Just clearing my throat. A lot of pollen in the air today."

"Sure…" Maggie stayed standing behind the other chair. She saw how they were caught in the narrow space but still couldn't imagine one man could hope to threaten two well-armed detectives. She felt her neck tingle again and a cool sensation pass through her brain, making it easier for her to size up the situation. Flashes of the room went through her mind, showing her what the room looked like from different angles, down to the details.

She kept her gaze on Winters, her lips pressed together in a straight line and let the images rapidly roll past. "You can wait outside." She said it as a command instead of a courtesy, making Taylor look up in surprise, concern passing over his face. Her fingers were tapping the top of her gun, her arm tense. "We've got it from here."

"Of course," said Winters, backing away. Maggie noted that he didn't look surprised at all.

"It's a trap," she said in a hushed tone to Taylor just before Winters took only a step back and cupped his hands in front of his chest, muttering something again, still too low to be heard.

"What kind of mumbo jumbo is he saying? He must be from Louisiana. I have folks from those parts. Can't understand a dang thing they say, either." Taylor shoved the chair back, hitting the desk and stood up, already drawing his gun. "Something's just not right here."

That was all he got out.

A dark blue bubble had formed in the curator's hands, filled with small bolts of lightning that grew as the bubble did, flashing and sparking. The sickly sweet smell of lavender was everywhere.

"What in the Sam Hill?" Taylor held up his gun, flanking Maggie to the right.

Maggie was bracing herself, not sure what was coming next. "Bernie, I could use an assist."

Taylor's brows knit together. "Bernie? Is that a safe word I don't know about?"

The storm grew inside the bubble, even as the bubble stretched until it was three feet wide, suddenly bursting and sending a shock wave, pulsating at the two detectives.

Maggie felt it hit her with a loud snap followed by crackling, lifting her off her feet. It all felt like it was happening in slow motion.

The wave of energy pushed her back, bending her even

as she resisted. She hit the back wall, knocking her head against the plaster as Taylor took out a monitor with his shoulder, rolling onto the table before hitting the floor. His gun was knocked out of his hand and he rested his head against the carpet, his eyes not focused on anything in particular.

Maggie slid down the wall, her hand clamping over her pocket, the wind knocked out of her and the air around her shimmering like blacktop on a hot summer day in Austin. Maggie reached for her gun and squinted through the pain and the thick, vibrating air, doing her best to aim at the curator who was busy constructing another bubble. She got off a shot, winging his right arm and bursting the bubble.

He let out a squeal even as the second wave of energy passed over her, weaker than the first but still enough to make her groggy. "Get up, get up!" She gritted her teeth and willed herself to get on her knees, putting out one foot and slapping her hand on the desk, leaning heavily as she shoved herself to a standing position. The gun still drawn in her other hand.

Winters opened his mouth and blew out a series of translucent bubbles as small metal balls appeared inside of them. The bubbles lined up quickly and started shooting at Maggie's direction, bursting as they hit her in the chest, the metal balls pushing her back down to a seated position on the floor and stunning her just enough to lose her grip on her gun.

She rolled on her side, pressing the compass against the floor, feeling the warmth through her pocket. It seemed to be warning her of something more.

Winters saw his chance and peeled Maggie's fingers back, wrestling away the gun. She clawed at his hand, straining to regain control, eliciting another yelp from him.

He pointed it at her head, swinging it back toward Taylor who was out cold and back at Maggie. There was a sheen of sweat across his face. "I have orders not to harm you. Well, nothing permanent at least. You have to realize, someone like you, that this is for the best. For our best, for all of humanity. We have to make sure the ship goes back to where it came from and we can all go back to paradise."

Maggie did her best to sit back up, feeling like she was high on something as the electric pulse still sizzled around her. "Why is it that comic book villains always have to lay out their plans? Where's the power point? I'm gonna need slides." Her words came out slightly slurred but determined.

Winters shook his head, annoyed. "Make jokes but it has to be done. Hand it over, come on." He held out his hand, shaking it, his voice cracking from the nerves.

Taylor was pushing himself into a seated position, slowly reaching for his gun a short distance away on the floor but Winters saw him and kicked the gun away. Maggie pushed against the wall, her teeth grinding from the effort. She could taste blood in her mouth, even as the room seemed to spin. *Damn, is it really spinning?*

"You know what I'm here for, just give it to me." Winters' voice sounded like a whine from a petulant, hairy-faced child.

"You want it, you come and get it," Maggie hissed, already balling up her fist. Winters seemed confused about what to do next, but he put the gun down as far from the two detectives as he could and blew out small bubbles that floated in the air between himself and Maggie. His wounded right arm hung at his side.

Maggie felt the cool trickle pass through her brain again, calming her down and she let her muscles relax. It felt like she was following instructions being given to her from someplace deep inside. Still, her hand was clenched by her side, waiting.

Watch the bubbles. You can do this. That's when she saw the pattern. *They're alive! Not just air and liquid.*

The bubbles moved and bobbed and swirled as Maggie did her best to focus her eyes and look for the pockets. *One, two, three, turns, three four five, turns.*

He reached out to search her just as she swung, picking her moment, her fist diving between the bubbles and making contact with his chin, sending him back. There was a surprised look on his face as his teeth clacked together and his head bobbed. The bubbles between them swirled into a chaotic ball, looking more like soap bubbles clinging to each other, a grey mist appearing inside of each one.

"No! Enough!" Winters spit out the words, cradling his jaw gingerly. The bubbles responded and broke apart, forming a thick, straight line, swiftly moving through the air and wrapping around Maggie's throat, squeezing tighter and tighter cutting off air.

She gagged, reaching up to crush the bubbles but instead felt a sharp sting. "Rule 54," she gasped. Still, she persisted, crushing them even as more appeared. Winters slipped in, patting her pockets and easily found the compass.

Maggie heard the sizzle as the compass burned his skin and smelled the acrid air. He pulled his hand back, his face twisted in pain as the rage built inside of him. He quickly pulled out a handkerchief and wrapped it around his hand, using his teeth to get it all the way around.

"Not... gonna... happen..." Maggie gasped out the words, determined to keep fighting even as the world grew darker.

Taylor got to his knees, his eyes still not completely focused and lunged for Winters who placed his heel in the center of Taylor's chest and shoved him backward.

He wasted no time dipping his hands back into Maggie's pocket even as her eyes started to roll back in her head, scooping out the compass. He ran for the door even as the bubbles already started to fade and pop against her skin and she gulped for air, struggling to stay awake, watching Winters escape.

She had lost the compass.

"Taylor, are you okay?"

He raised his hand in the air and smiled grimly, trying to reassure her. "What the hell was that?"

"A new kind of reality."

"You're going to have to explain that one to me."

"I'll do my best, but I'm not sure I get any of it yet, either."

"Were we just attacked by freakin' killer bubbles? You can do the paperwork for this one." Taylor got himself to a seated position and rubbed the back of his neck, groaning.

"On second thought, you aren't one for bending the truth and this could get us sidelined. I'll take care of it."

"You do that." *I'll be hunting that compass.*

Frank Winters wasted no time rushing across town to the Galaxy Cafe on the west side of town. He parked his car in the crowded parking lot by the karate studio and did his best to walk in like nothing was amiss. He had managed to stop the bleeding from his arm, the bullet had gone through and through and he still had the handkerchief wrapped around his burned hand.

He held his phone in his burned hand, considering calling Simon again, but he didn't want to anger him. He had said he didn't care, just drop off the compass and then take care of things. Winters had barely enough time to change his jacket into something that lacked bloodstains.

Simon liked his routine and there was very little that could get him to veer from it.

The Galaxy Cafe was part of his routine. Twice a week for an early dinner. It was one of Simon's favorite haunts. He liked to sit by the window and eat his favorite, a Buddha bowl. Steamed kale, lentils, sweet potato and brown rice. It was his idea of fast food. On days he was feeling good he'd even add a little hot sauce.

Frank came bustling inside, pushing past someone holding the door with his right hand resting in his pocket to give his arm some support. The pain was giving him a headache. He came and stood by the table, not sure what to do.

"Sit down, you're attracting attention." Simon looked up, a flicker of annoyance across his face. "Let me see it."

Winters slid into the chair and gingerly pulled out the compass. It had cooled and was easier to handle but the skin on his palm was blistered and it was painful to do anything with it. Simon watched him, taking it all in, assessing the situation like any good forensics specialist. He opened his hand and waited for Winters to drop the compass into it, almost smiling when at last, he had it. "This one small piece of machinery is key to everything." He held it closer, looking at the five needles, admiring everything about it. "Elementa invenient me. Ostende mihi viam. Ignis ventus aqua terra." Find me the elements. Show me the path. Fire wind water earth. He waited anxiously, eager to finally get answers, but the compass just sat there, the needles swinging loosely in the case. He held the compass gently in his hand, shaking with anger as he resisted the urge to smash it against the tabletop. "Damn it!" he hissed under his breath.

"What's wrong? Did I get the wrong thing?" Winters was breathing heavily, his bandaged hand wrapped around a cold glass of water.

"Believe it or not, not everything is about you, Frank. It appears we only got half of what we needed. It's going to take the damn Elemental to make the pretty toy work. I'm going to have to get Maggie Parker to assist or die trying. Found the compass, still need to save the world."

"That's not going to be easy. She has trust issues."

"She just needs persuading, of one kind or another. It can't be helped. We're going to do whatever it takes for the greater good."

CHAPTER NINE

Maggie drove Taylor home, he had refused to go to the hospital. He said it would be too hard to explain. "Besides, two cops walking into an emergency room would draw too much attention. The Captain would find out in no time and want to know what happened. Let me sleep it off and then I can come up with a plausible explanation."

"Great, then you can tell me."

Taylor looked over at Maggie trying to gingerly hold the wheel despite her swollen fingertips. "I assume you have your own reasons for not heading to the hospital."

"About the same as yours."

"And a few more?"

Maggie shrugged, too tired and aching all over to come up with something clever.

She waited till he climbed wearily out of the car and up his front walk while Claire, his wife waited at the door, a look of concern on her face.

She watched him shake his head and attempt to shrug as he made his way inside and Lanie waved to Maggie before shutting the door.

"I have no idea how to explain this one," she whispered, pulling slowly away from the curb.

What hurt even worse was losing the compass. Maggie didn't like losing on a typical day with much lower stakes. "I don't even know what the stakes are in this game. That needs to change," she muttered, wincing as a car cut in front of her and she cut the wheel to avoid their back bumper, the blisters on her fingers making contact with the steering wheel.

Bubbles appeared across the highway floating and bobbing gently. Faces in the other cars were smiling and pointing, admiring how the sunlight was creating small rainbows inside of them. Only Maggie was grimacing and narrowing her gaze, bracing herself for whatever might come next. She could smell strawberries everywhere.

The wind seemed to blow the bubbles back toward her car, surrounding it before getting sucked into the front of the grill. They came pouring out of every crack in the dashboard, gathering together and reconstituting themselves on the seat next to her.

"Son of a…" Maggie yelled out, whipping the wheel to the right, trying to get to the side of the road, even as she cried out in pain. A pale image appeared inside of the bubbles as Maggie brought the car to a stop, even as a white Hyundai blew its horn, angrily shaking his hand over his head as he sped past her.

Maggie lunged at the bubbles, not giving them a chance

to fully form, ignoring rule number 54 and risking further injury, but it was too late. Bernie was sitting there in the seat, sputtering as he fended off her attack, his eyes wide. He swatted at her hands, startled as she pulled back in pain.

"What the hell happened? You were out of my sight for less than a day." He slapped his forehead, exasperated as he took in her entire appearance.

"You should see the other guy." She made a weak smile, leaning on the steering wheel for a moment, closing her eyes as she let out a deep sigh. The day had started with a bullet headed toward her forehead with a side trip to Narnia and was bookended neatly in a magical fight with choking bubbles. She lifted her head and looked him straight in the eyes. "I lost the compass." Maggie was never one to avoid anything. "I don't even know who or what he was. Not a Kashgar, at least he didn't look like a gnome, no offense."

"Why would you say, no offense? What's the offensive part?" he grumbled, gesturing at his body. "Kashgars, the tall bastards, blend in better than we do. Could have definitely been one of them." He made a loud tsk, tsk and hesitated, rubbing his chin.

"What? What are you not telling me?"

Bernie threw up his hands. "I can see you haven't quite grasped your situation yet. Not your fault. You have no guide, and yet you're an Elemental." He words came out in a whistle through his front teeth.

"So I've heard."

"You're not only an Elemental, you're *the* Elemental. There may be a few different factions hunting for you."

"The Elemental, what does that even mean? Hunting? Factions? Keep this simple and explain."

"That's a lot of questions. Okay, hunting may be a little too strong. How about looking?"

Maggie gave him a cold, steady look. "Have you seen my hands? They look like steamed dumplings. They're doing more than looking. They touched the merchandise." She twisted around in her seat, cars slowing down as the rush hour set in, some peering inside with nothing better to do than imagine what was going on inside the El Camino.

"Worse part is I should have been able to take the guy," she growled. "No problem, game over. Instead, I got throttled by a bunch of bubbles. My partner, a veteran cop easily topping out over two hundred pounds got his bell rung and something supposedly vital to an entire planet got swiped from my pocket like it was lunch money." She was doing her best to keep her voice low and even, but it was a strain and she was starting to yell.

"Boy, this is gonna make my next statement really awkward." Bernie sputtered, blowing small bubbles that turned into tiny iridescent fireflies, winking a pale yellow glow before quickly fading. The faint scent of strawberries was only there for a moment.

Maggie arched an eyebrow and leaned back against her car door. "Try me…"

"Wooo boy, you're not gonna make this easy. Fine, here goes. I need your help getting the compass back."

Maggie let out a snort and gave him a crooked smile that didn't make it all the way up to her eyes. "I'm not going to help you get the compass back."

Bernie started to sputter faster as bubbles spilled out in rapid succession, and tiny fireflies filled the car. A car slowed down even further to get a better look as the bugs blinked their lights and only sped up after the car behind him laid on their horn.

He gulped and pressed his lips together sheepishly, waiting for the fireflies to fade. "That happens when I get nervous. Some people like it."

"Are those even real?"

"They could be." He hiccupped and two last fireflies erupted, blinking a yellow light before popping in mid-air. "I need your help. I don't think I can do this one on my own and there's too much riding on it."

"I didn't say I wasn't going to find the damn thing. I'm not going to help you." She held up her sore and swollen hands. "You are going to help me."

Bernie let out a deep sigh, his chest heaving. "Okay, great, I can live with that."

"Why such a turnaround? You were pretty anxious not to involve me before and you were full of attitude."

"Things have changed. There was a meeting of all the mechanics and I had to take a quick break. While I was gone, Jack made sure to nominate me to take care of you. Seems there's a general feeling I botched the whole thing from the get go."

"The break in…"

"That's the thing they mentioned." He tapped his chest. "I don't agree, mind you, but we're a union, a brethren," his voice got louder, his confidence returning for a moment. "Got to go with the conscience of the group."

"They threatened to kick you out, didn't they?"

He looked sheepish, lacing his hands together under his belly. "Something like that. There may have been mention of being permanently assigned to fixing the Earth's plumbing system that is Rotorua, New Zealand. Smell of rotten eggs from those steam vents stays with you for days! Truth is, that's one of the ship's natural sewer systems."

"Good to know it took a global crapper for you to want to take my side. No wonder you're playing nice."

"Enjoy it, this is harder than the time I had to be a giraffe for a few days." He shook his head, squeezing his eyes shut as he rubbed his neck. "There was a problem at the National Zoo, and some concern over not having enough giraffes if we do ever get this ship moving again. I mean, conjuring a bubble to make my neck do that..." He raised his chin, widening his hands vertically, further and further apart. "I mean, you can imagine."

Maggie tilted her head to the side, watching him. "Are you about done?"

He clamped his mouth shut and brought his hands together, a scowl on his face. "I thought we were sharing! Isn't that how you Peabrains like to bond? A lot of talking about feelings?"

"You're in Texas and we have better things to do. This is how it's going to go. You're going to answer a lot of my questions and that's going to help me formulate a plan."

Bernie narrowed his eyes, rubbing his chin. "Rotorua, hang out with you. Tough call."

"Three seconds…"

"Fine, I'll answer your questions. Fire away, and just so we're clear, Texan, use your words, not your gun."

"I'm keeping my options open. First thing I need to

know is why I got all the way into my twenties before anyone noticed I'm apparently the key to figuring out a world-sized problem."

"That was the Kashgars, tall bastards. In their haste to burn down the Library at Alexandria, they failed to save the Elemental records. It was all destroyed and with it the identities of every Elemental, along with a few operating manuals that really would have come in handy. Try taming a tornado without any instructions."

"You can fix the weather?"

The traffic picked up along the highway behind them, moving faster.

"Oh sure, after all, this giant thing is nothing more than an oversized organic ship. My uncle said it was a snap, back in the day." He snapped his fingers in the air, a bubble emerging with a small tornado inside, surrounded by tiny flying debris. He snapped his fingers again and the tornado fell apart, replaced by a blue sky and soft, cumulus clouds. The top of a giraffe lumbered through the bubble on its way to somewhere unseen. "Until that fire, this whole ship was just what it was supposed to be; a regular paradise for all the passengers and cargo. Since then, the mechanics," he pointed his thumb at his chest, "my people, have been regular geniuses coming up with different ways to fix things without spare parts, not to mention stuff we didn't see coming."

He threw his hands up, getting worked and pointing his finger at Maggie. "That part would be all you guys. Peabrains may not remember they're magical but boy, they are inventive and you all like to move things around.

Rabbits where they don't belong, fish in the wrong rivers and kudzu! Don't get me started."

"I feel we're a little off topic. Tell me why the compass is so important, why I'm so important."

"I am doing just that. You see, to get this you're going to have to see the big picture. Come here, take my hand. Don't worry, I washed them yesterday. I do it every Tuesday whether I need to or not."

Maggie wrinkled her nose but took his hand anyway. "Gently…" The blisters were still throbbing.

"Oh yeah, about those." Bernie turned in his seat to face her the best he could and gently took both of her hands into his, opening his mouth to make a perfect 'o'. Pale purple bubbles the size of a baseball squeezed out and drifted lazily down to their joined hands, sliding across the surface of their skin.

Maggie's eyes widened and she looked up at Bernie. The pain was easing.

"I know, right?" Bernie smiled, opening his mouth again to release more bubbles. "No one can remember how to heal more than burns like this or a pretty good gash."

"I can feel them moving around inside of my skin."

"Your kind would call it technology I suppose, these days. I mean you have figured out how to build an internet. We call it ancient magic. Maybe in the end it's the same thing."

Maggie took in an easy, deep breath and felt the throbbing subside down to nothing. She realized how tired she was but shook it off. There was too much to learn and maybe not enough time. Someone else had the compass.

"Tell me about the compass."

"Done?" He let go of one of her hands and stood back, still holding tight. "First, I have to show you a few things."

"Are we about to fly?"

"Don't be ridiculous. That's just in comic books."

"I fell through the Earth but flying is off the table."

"Pay attention, here we go."

CHAPTER TEN

Maggie felt a tingle along the back of her neck and a thin, cold ribbon of energy push through her brain. The interior of the El Camino disappeared and she found herself standing on a wide-open plain in Africa as a herd of gazelles ran past, leaping over a narrow gorge. She could feel the wind on her face and feel the ground shake under her feet. The earthy smell of hundreds of gazelles running past filled the air.

"This is what the Earth looked like back when we first approached the sun."

Maggie felt her head swim and her stomach lurch as the icy thread spread through her head again and the images stretched and changed to an icy river. A grizzly bear was leaning over the side, swiping at trout. Maggie and Bernie were standing on the far bank on the edge of a pine forest and Maggie could hear the trees creak as they swayed in the cold wind. The scent of pine bark was overwhelming and comforting. She reached out with her foot and kicked a frozen pine cone and was startled to feel it connect and the pine cone skitter across the ground. Her entire body shivered from the cold and she let out a breath to watch it turn into steam.

She turned to look behind her, peering through the trees but they seemed to stretch on forever.

The ground shifted again, and her knees buckled for just a moment as Bernie squeezed her hand tighter. She looked over at him. "You're sharing your energy," she said in a hushed tone. Her hand warmed, the sensation spreading up her arm and throughout her body as the images changed and stretched.

The smell of saltwater and fish hit her in the face, and she breathed in deeply, remembering time spent in the gulf with her parents when she was small. They were standing on a sandy beach, clear blue water lapping around their feet. A pod of spinner dolphins emerged from the water, twirling around and dropping back beneath the surface.

Maggie gasped, letting out a spontaneous squeal of delight, surprising herself as she felt the water seep into her shoes. But before she could say anything, the location changed, and she was in the middle of a tomato farm under the hot sunlight.

"Taste one, go ahead."

"I thought this was from a long time ago."

"It was and it isn't. You're not time traveling, you're seeing one of the memories that the ship holds, but it's not the same as our memories. They're real for just a moment at a time, to be enjoyed and then they vanish. It's like a vast record of everything that ever existed on the ship."

"Everything?"

"I know where you're going with that and that's rule

number sixty-two. We don't visit the dead. All you'd be able to see is what happened, you can't talk to them. No good has ever come from taking a trip like that. It sucks people in like glue. There was that incident back in 1934 and I think that guy is still stuck staring at the past."

Maggie narrowed her gaze, shading her eyes from the sun. The deep, pungent smell of the tomato vines made her relax and take a deep breath. She felt herself getting pulled further into the Earth's memory.

"Go ahead, try one."

She heard Bernie's voice like it was in the distance. "Sink your teeth into one."

Maggie reached out and moved several thick vines aside to find a fat, deep red tomato hanging low to the ground. She pulled it off and held it up to her nose, breathing deeply, before opening her mouth wide and taking a bite. The juice ran down her chin and dripped onto her shirt as she chewed the bite of tomato, filling her cheeks. She swallowed and went to take another bite just as they were pulled away, sent back to the interior of the El Camino. Her mouth closed around a puff of air even as her eyes widened in surprise.

There was no longer anything in her hand, but she could smell the vines everywhere.

She smacked her lips, still tasting the tomato. "That was so real."

"It was, and it wasn't. You experienced it, it gave you something, fed your senses in every way."

"But all I'm left with is the memory."

"Yes, like all the rest of life. You know, this was the early version of entertainment for all the passengers. A way to go anywhere, try anything at a moment's notice. A Peabrain or an elf or wizard could forget everything and try out a different part of the ship without leaving their home. It was better than going to the movies."

"I'll say." She looked down at her shoes expecting to see sand. "And we forgot all of this," she said in hushed tones. "How is that even possible?"

"A story for another day. That's more staring at the past. There's enough on our plate already."

Maggie shook her head and turned back in her seat, looking out the windshield. "We need to get going. Can't sit by the side of the road all day." She looked at Bernie. "Was that the rest of the Alice in Wonderland world tour?"

"For now, it's plenty. You get the idea. This organic ship is a living, breathing piece of machinery that can do amazing things. That was just a small twinkling of what I could show you."

Maggie started up the El Camino and looked over her left shoulder, pulling back into traffic.

Bernie opened her glove compartment and rummaged around inside of it. "You have anything to eat in here? I'm starving."

"You can't make something to eat with your bubbles?"

"Bubbles are good for healthy food, not my specialty. Give me a nice taquito or queso dip. The bubbles don't seem to know how to make that and believe me I've tried." He slapped his thigh with a laugh that ended in a grimace. "I ended up with a bowl of spaghetti squash and tomatoes."

"That's not bad…"

"Not exactly good either. There's nothing," he said,

pulling out an old green M&M from a dark corner of the seat and popping it in his mouth. "Mmmm, still chocolate."

Maggie glanced over, wrinkling her nose as she changed lanes. "Barely. Tell me more about the compass and the Elementals."

"There's fire, wind, water, soil and you, the one who guides them all. Each of you represents a vital part of the ship and together you make up the basic elements that were built into her. Hence the name. *You* are the most important one. With just a couple of the elements in place plus you, we could heal something on the ship…"

"Like a hurricane."

Bernie clapped his hands together, sliding to the front of his seat. "You were listening!"

Maggie pumped the brakes as the car in front of her hit theirs hard, sending the gnome toward the dashboard. He put out his arms to brace himself, scowling.

"Put your seat belt on," she said.

The Huldu grunted, sliding the belt over his ample stomach. "You know, I can motivate out of here if worse comes to worse."

"And tell your clan you left me to die. Sounds like that would lead to something even worse than tending to the world's crapper." Maggie sat back, resting one arm on the edge of the door and her hand on the top of the wheel. "You have to think these things through all the way."

"Not the first time I've heard that. Where was I? The Elementals. With just three of the Elementals in place plus you we could probably fix the ship enough to pull out of the sun's orbit. That's the theory anyway. But if you're not there…" He blew a raspberry. "No can go. The compass doesn't even work for anyone but the rightful Elemental. Right now, that's you."

"But it wasn't always me."

"Oh no, there's only one per generation and it doesn't pass to the next until well…" He drew his finger along his neck. "We always know when one has passed, even if we didn't know who it was. There would be something unusual like a row of tornadoes if it was a wind Elemental or a sink hole the size of a house would suddenly open up if it was the dirt Elemental."

Maggie turned down Pressler and pulled in her driveway. "You staying or are you about to dissolve into a pile of bubbles?"

"I'm here for the duration. Not to worry, I'm quiet and tend to like to keep to myself. I do have a short list for the grocery store." He pulled a list out of the pocket of his green overalls. He was still wearing the same green sweater. "Easy stuff, and this way I won't have to bother you for food. All ready to eat, well, except for the ramen. Love those little cups. And the frozen pizzas but I can work a microwave." Bernie counted each item off on his fingers. "Oh, and the coffee but I assume you have a way to make that too."

Maggie reached over and pushed down his hand, taking the list. "Queso, no surprise. I don't see chips on here. You eat it by itself? Okay, okay, no judgment."

"Just a little side eye."

"Twizzlers, malt balls, Funyuns. This isn't really food. Gum?"

"That no judgment didn't last long. The Earth agrees with you apparently. This is all food of sorts. I mean it took stuff from the ship to make it all. Okay, refined stuff and maybe a lab. Oooh, don't forget the Pop-Tarts and Hot Pockets. That covers two different meals." He tapped the list, eagerly looking up at her.

"Fine, what do I know about what a Huldu eats." Maggie opened her car door and got out, walking by a young redbud tree in the front yard. The tree branches rustled as she passed, bending in her direction.

Bernie got out of the car and followed behind her. Maggie turned and walked back to the car as the branches settled back into place. She narrowed her gaze and stared at the tree a moment before walking back up the driveway, more slowly this time. Again, the branches swayed ever so slightly toward her.

"What the hell?" Maggie stood there with her hands on her hips.

Bernie rolled his eyes and walked past her, muttering, "You're waking up to the magic inside of you. Of course the trees would all know. Your average Peabrain knows the trees can talk to each other. That's basic information." He threw his hands up in the air, still walking toward the door as Maggie walked backward behind him, watching the branches slowly drop. Her mouth opened in surprise as she saw the branches sway in nearby trees like a rolling wave down the street.

Bernie turned and waited for her by the steps. "The word's out, sister. The Earth knows you're the Elemental and the ship is spreading the word. It's a good thing. The Earth will instinctively do its best to protect you. I mean, there are limits, mind you." He shrugged and put out his hands. "That's why I'm assigned to be with you, at least for the next few years."

Maggie heard the word *years* and almost said something, but a memory was just taking shape in her mind, capturing her attention. She walked back by the tree and saw the branches sway. "I remember," she whispered, her eyes moving back and forth between the tree in front of her and the other trees that lined the street. "Dad showed me."

She was so young when he first took her to meet the trees, introducing them by name, making a game out of it. "I had to be only four years old. He said, they were all my friends. I remember the branches moving." It felt like her head was swimming as her eyes glistened. She slowly walked over to the young redbud and put out her hand, touching the bark with her fingertips. "That hum, I've felt that before." She turned and looked at Bernie who was walking over to her side. "I think I felt it when I was little. I know I felt it when I held the compass."

"Makes sense. You are a connection between the ship and everything the ship helps to create. That's the energy of the ship you're feeling. Her energy's moving through you."

The tree's branches rustled, and Maggie watched as one by one, trees rustled in response on down the street, passing into the distance.

Maggie felt an ache in her chest, longing for the memory to stay with her. "He was teaching me," she said, as a tear fell down her cheek. Small leaves from the tree fell over her head, dropping onto her shoulders.

"If you're close enough to them, the trees will feel what you feel. It feels your pain."

Maggie felt a shiver go down her spine and a cool thread of energy pass through her head. She felt the longing pass from her chest and a sense of peace came over her, the humming traveling down her arm and into the tree. Again, the branches rustled, sending out a signal that passed down the line as the sunlight faded in the sky. Maggie smiled, keeping her hand still. "They're telling each other, all is well. I can feel it."

"I tell you, I've been a Huldu going on two centuries and this still gets me." Bernie pulled a stained rag out of his back pocket and wiped his face. "You have anything to eat? Maybe a drink?"

Maggie ignored him and shut her eyes, feeling the energy flow through her, a crooked smile coming across her face. "He was trying to teach me."

"Well of course he was teaching you. It was part of his duties. The trees would have been at the top of the list. I told you, basic even for Peabrains. Trees can talk to each other from miles away, even share water or food through their roots. They have their own kind of magic."

Maggie removed her hand and felt the hum subside and the energy seep back somewhere deep inside of her. She was still left with a sense of calm. "For a second it was like he was back by my side, holding my hand."

"That's the Earth sharing its memory with you. Let go of it. Like I said, you can get stuck there." He took her by the hand, grounding her as the calm faded. "I know, sorry about that but it's necessary. You're in danger and the compass is missing. Keep your head in the very deadly game. The Kashgars will want to use you to get the ship moving, but in the wrong direction."

"I don't think a Kashgar has the compass. I can't believe I'm going to use this word, but I think a Peabrain took it." Maggie stood on her lawn, pressing her lips together, looking around at her house and the street she had known all of her life. Across the street Mrs. Feitig waved to her as she got her mail out of the mailbox. "This is where we belong. We need to stay in this orbit."

"Well, maybe."

"No, really. For better or worse, this has become our home. It's not a ship to us, it's home. I'll defend it, if that's what we're talking about, but I need more information." Maggie put her hands on her hips and stood up straighter, her chin up. She looked at Bernie, determined. "It's the only way I'll cooperate with this whole thing. Otherwise, I find the compass on my own and I destroy it. If you can't find it, you can't use it to move the Earth anywhere else."

"A little bit of extortion, but I get it." Bernie rubbed his hands together. "I can work with it. Hell, we've been here this long, a few hundred more years won't matter. We'll negotiate."

"No, we won't."

"Table that for later. I can see you're fired up. Let me grab some chow from your kitchen and there's something special I want to show you." Bernie headed for the stairs, climbing to the porch.

"Show me now."

"Come on, lady, give me a little food, some nectar of the gods. A little Lucky Charms. My cousin, Herbie loves those. I'd even take a bagel at this point. No salad, I can make that myself."

Maggie was already walking back to the car, her hand on the door.

"Fine!" Bernie climbed down the stairs and looked around to see if anyone was watching. The street was empty. "Can't afford to break any more rules today. Don't need another oversight committee meeting about what Bernie's done wrong this year." He brushed his hands together quickly, increasing the speed until his hands were a blur. Just as suddenly, he pulled them apart creating an oversized bubble that found its way to Maggie, enveloping her.

"Bernie, you're gonna have to warn me before you pull these stunts." The bubble encased her as the sounds of birds and the wind muffled and the light dimmed. "Hey, aren't you coming with me?"

"I'll be right behind you. No worries."

CHAPTER ELEVEN

His voice trailed off as the last of the day's light came back and she found herself standing outside of the main library in downtown Austin behind the dumpsters. The bubble popped and the sound returned as a man in dirty cargo pants and three layers of sweat shirts ambled past her pushing a shopping cart. "More bubbles," he muttered, walking past her. "Just look away, Johnny, it's not real."

Bernie appeared by her side, the bubble making a distinct 'pop' as the man twisted around and stared at the gnome.

"Not sure what it says that I keep dreaming up a small, ugly old man for a friend."

Bernie arched an eyebrow. "Right back at you."

"The girl's an improvement. You got any food, imaginary friend?"

"Give him whatever it was you took from my house," said Maggie, nudging Bernie in the shoulder.

"Who says I took anything?"

"I'm a pretty good detective, Bernie. You sent me ahead so you could magically pilfer from my house. Do it. Give it to him."

Bernie let out a resigned sigh. "Fine, but I'm going to need food pretty soon. I can't go forever without a little MSG and sugar." He pulled a bag of Milano cookies from inside of his overalls and handed them over.

"Oooh, chocolate mint. My favorite. See you back here later?"

"He knows you, doesn't he? This isn't your first trip here."

"Slim, here has an amazing knack for being at the dumpster just when I arrive. Come on, this isn't why I brought you here."

Slim called after Bernie. "Bring a Happy Meal the next time, but this time make sure it's still warm."

Maggie smiled, catching up with Bernie as they headed toward the main doors. "You're taking care of him. No need to comment."

They went into the lobby and Maggie passed through the metal detectors, setting off a loud beeping noise. She emptied her pockets into a yellow plastic bowl and tried again, with the same results. She took off her coat and handed it over as a guard patted her down, finding nothing. At last she was allowed to past through, but not without a few long looks from others.

Bernie walked through with no problem and caught up to her. "We're going to the second floor, follow me. Don't let the metal detector get to you. More odd things are going to keep happening to you now. Your peabrain is waking up and the element buried inside of you is activated. No going back."

"Should make getting on planes fun."

They got to the second floor and he took her by the elbow, passing through the stacks to a back wall, where he kept on walking, easily pulling her through the wall to a hidden room. Maggie spun around, catching her bearings. "That was so cool! What just happened?"

Bernie rolled his eyes. "Basic magic. You're too easily impressed." He went to a large purple tome set up on an easel in front of tall wooden shelves filled with old books. "The mayor is an Elf and we go way back. When they started building the new library he offered to build this room. It's a secure place to keep what we've managed to write down since the great fire. No Kashgar can get in here, those tall bastards."

Maggie looked over his shoulder at the book. "That's a family tree." She touched the thin, gold lines that connected the names.

"This is my family line." Bernie puffed out his chest, smiling. "Huldus tracing all the way back to when the ship was first boarded.

"There's over a hundred names. You go all the way back to…" She squinted, reading out the name at the top of the tree. "Erie."

"Erie was the head of all the Huldus on this ship and the one who came up with the idea to break apart the main parts of the engine. He fought Peres, the leader of the Kashgars and saved everything on the Earth with his quick thinking."

Maggie smiled at him. "You come from a very noble line of gnomes."

Bernie blushed and sputtered, small bubbles erupting from his mouth and tiny fireflies dancing in the air. "Okay, enough of that. Not why we're here." He turned the pages carefully, scanning the ancient text. "Yeah, yeah, here it is. Look at this. This is why I brought you here. It's all that's left about the Earth's own Elemental and the compass. That would now be you."

Maggie leaned over, rubbing the words with her finger, even though she couldn't read the ancient hieroglyphics. "This was about one of my ancestors."

"All the way down to you. This book can't leave here but we can take some of the rules and spells and try them out. I'll tutor you into being an Elemental. Sorry, but it's gonna have to do. Look at this, it says you should be able to work a few spells. So much to learn! Try saying, regurus abilinum."

"Regurus abilinum." Maggie's body shook and bubbles appeared in her palms, changing into flowers that dropped onto the floor, one right after the other. She tried shaking her hands but that only made the flowers drop faster. "Tell me you have an off switch on this, Bernie!"

"That was impressive even if it's not exactly what was supposed to happen! You have some powers, kid. I'm looking, I'm looking. Somewhere… somewhere…" He flipped the delicate pages as fast as he dared, running his finger up and down the symbols, muttering pieces of spells.

The flowers continued to fall, piling up around Maggie's ankles. The scent of magnolias filled the room with a sickening sweet smell that was making her nauseous.

"Killing weeds, fending off bears, helping trolls, finding mushrooms... Ah, here it is." He smiled and tapped the book.

"Can you celebrate later? I've become my own florist over here." Maggie lifted her hands in frustration, creating a cascade of blossoms.

"You have to admit, it's kind of pretty." Bernie plucked a blossom and smelled it, stuffing it into his pocket. "Right, okay, excalipis abilinum no more."

Maggie felt a warm tingling in her hands and the last of the flowers appeared with some of their petals missing, fading into bubbles and harmlessly popping.

"Maybe we need a little more study before we try another spell."

Bernie nodded, kicking away some of the flowers. "I see your point. This is more of a long-term project. No quick fixes."

"Tell me what you meant when you yelled, I was living on borrowed time."

"Oooh that." He pursed his lips, twiddling his thumbs. "To be honest, I don't know. All I have are the old stories, which are open to interpretation."

"If you're not going to be straight with me, I'm leaving, just as soon as I find a door." Maggie pushed at the wall where they came in, but nothing happened.

"The Earth could sense at any given moment you're not supposed to still be here and, shall we say, adjust appropriately."

"You mean, kill me off."

"That's one way of putting it. Seems a little harsh but okay." Bernie scratched the top of his head, wrinkling his nose.

"My death would seem harsh to me."

"I can see that. Good news, the earth may not notice this particular imbalance. Here's the tricky part. You're the basic Elemental that the earth can communicate with, which means she may see you as necessary and weigh things out. I'm not saying the ship thinks." Bernie squinted his eyes, raising his shoulders to his ears. "But there's a kind of intelligence that weighs what's best for the greater number. It was built into the giant organism to help protect the voyage. She may see you as necessary for the greater good."

"But if she doesn't, if the compass is lost forever, poof." Maggie felt a tightness in her chest just thinking about the prospect. *Mom and Diana. Do I warn them?*

Bernie had turned back to the book and was distracted, turning more pages and muttering words. "Here's what we need right now. Yeah, that should do it, well at least get us started."

"Give me more nouns, Bernie. I sense we're off on another adventure and this time I'd like some warning."

"We have the beginning of a plan to locate the compass. A way to track it that requires you. See here," he said, running his finger along the raised symbols, "the Elemental of the compass can draw on the energy of the Earth and follow the vibrations straight to the compass."

"Bernie, that's great but I have no idea how to do that. Just because I was able to get in touch with one tree doesn't mean I've mastered anything. I wouldn't even know where to start. Take off my shoes, stand in the dirt, maybe."

"Interesting idea but the dirt doesn't talk back. It's just dirt, come on, and you're not that Elemental. Let's start with the obvious. We'll go talk to the trees and see if they will talk back to us."

Bernie read the last lines of the page he had been reading and grimaced, looking around the room. "Yeah, that's where it is. Hang on." He went to a shelf in the third row and reached up on his toes, his fingertips grazing a wooden box.

"Let me help." Maggie walked down the short aisle and reached up, easily reaching the box. She gave the Huldu a crooked smile as he grumbled under his breath about Peabrains and tall handsome bastards.

Bernie took the box from her, cradling it in his short, stocky arms and walked over to a small wooden table, laying it down. He waved his hand over the top, muttering, "Exegis be mine." The brass lock on the front popped up and the top loosened. He easily lifted the top and revealed a brass sextant that fit in the middle of his large palm. "We're good to go."

"What is that?"

"The backup plan just in case the compass was ever lost. You should learn that about the Huldus. We're all mechanics, which means we're practical and resourceful and always have another plan."

CHAPTER TWELVE

Bernie pulled Maggie through the wall and back into the library, still tugging on her hand as they went down the stairs. He hurried along, giving a nod here and there to some of the people they passed. Maggie turned, looking back at each one that he chose to acknowledge looking for the common thread, but couldn't see it.

She almost tripped on a stair, craning her neck to look back at a tall, elegant man in a cashmere jacket who gave a curt nod in reply to Bernie.

"Hey, watch where you're going. Rule number two! I can't use magic right here in the lobby to float you over the floor," he hissed.

"You know a lot of people, Bernie. I don't get it. I've lived in Austin my entire life and I don't know this many people wandering through a library on a weeknight."

"What? Oh, that." He gave a snort of laughter and stopped for a moment. "I'll give you one short lesson right here that might prove useful. Come stand right here and look around at everyone you see. Not everybody is actually a Peabrain. Some are elves or witches or wizards, your occasional fae and a few other magicals. The little lady behind the counter tugging at her pantyhose is an overweight pixie. Don't look at me like that. This isn't even the weirdest thing I've said to you today."

Maggie looked at each of them, looking for signs of magic. "I got nothing."

"Of course you do. Rule number two applies to all magicals who were on this voyage. A Peabrain that's woke is a little tricky. You have enough magic to be dangerous but no knowledge on how to use it, and we can only help but so much. Each case has to feel their way on their own. It's kind of funny if you think about it. Things blow up or get sent to a glacier, or some random street corner. You should see the gag reel Jack and I have underground. Too soon?"

Maggie took in a few deep breaths, letting them out slowly. Her entire body ached from fighting off too many things and taking in way too much all in one day. "When I got up this morning, my biggest concern was whether or not I'd beat Taylor to the Krispy Kreme doughnuts with the Nutella inside."

"Those are good, and please note that parts of this day have been downright fun. Now focus, I'm trying to teach you something. All of these magicals are using bubbles to hide who they are. Simple trick and simple to spot. Concentrate and at the same time let go."

"Do the opposite of each at the same time."

"Exactly." Bernie nodded, relieved Maggie was getting it.

"I'll rub my belly and tap my head for good measure."

"If you think it'll help, but I don't see how. Start already, I need to eat something, and we have a little work left to do."

"I could use a bath and a soft bed." Maggie felt her eyelids droop from weariness. *Shake it off. You need to prove you're useful to the Earth and that's going to take a compass.* "Okay, here we go." She shook out her arms and shut her eyes, breathing in through her nose and out through her mouth. *Let go, let go, let go. Make sure and stop for cream on the way home. Nope, that's not working. Okay, let's do it. Billions are counting on me.* A giggle escaped her, surprising her. *That's new. I could save billions. Can't even figure out a date.* Another giggle escaped her. *Too tired and hungry.*

"Focus on a memory of something you liked."

Bernie's voice sounded like it was coming from somewhere far away. *Being at the beach and watching her sister, Diana dancing in the waves, laughing. She was so happy.* She folded her arms across her chest and stretched her back just as a tingle spread across her neck and a cool, soothing thread of energy spread through her head. *There it is.*

She opened her eyes and focused on letting it go and leaving a space for it to stay. As long as she didn't think about it at all and just noticed the energy was there, it was working.

"You've got it! I can tell! Okay, put out an intention into your mind. Let it know that you want to see who's magical and who's not."

Maggie didn't say a word, not sure if she could speak and hold onto the energy. She kept focusing on her breathing, noticing the presence of the cool energy in her head and turned to look around the large open room in the library.

The librarian who was still trying to adjust her tight pantyhose had pointy ears peeking out of her hair and luminescent wings fluttering from her back. Her eyes glowed when she looked up at Maggie and she smiled and waved. Maggie gave a crooked smile but kept looking around, not sure she should move too much. A mother with two small children looked perfectly normal except for the pale white skin that almost glowed and the silver hair that caught the light.

"That's a witch," whispered Bernie. "Somewhere in that book bag is a wand. Look at the man you saw earlier on the stairs."

Coming down the stairs was the same elegantly dressed man who had nodded at Bernie. His ears were now pointed, and his eyebrows rose on the ends. He looked more closely at Maggie as he passed her and gave a slow nod. "Good evening, Peabrain," he said with respect.

All over the library dotted in between the human beings who were reading quietly were different magicals of every kind minding their own business, going about their day.

"Those human beings, they don't know there's a small peabrain that could just wake up one day and flood them with magic."

"No, a Peabrain kind of glows with a pale blue aura. See any of those?"

Maggie looked around. "Not a one."

"You're still kind of relatively rare. The only kind of magicals this doesn't work on are Kashgars, tall handsome bastards!" Bernie pounded his fist into his palm. "They pretty much look the same, either way. But there are other things that will tell you if you're looking at one of those traitors."

Maggie looked at Bernie. "Kashgars." The magic slipped away from her at the mention of the group that wanted her dead. Her mind started to put together a plan, stepping into the middle of a problem, no longer observing. She shook her head. "This isn't easy."

"It'll get easier. It's not about doing as much as it is allowing. Tough for a Peabrain. Come on, lesson over. Let's go track that compass and keep you above the ground. I mean…"

"I know what you meant. Not six feet under."

They headed back to the dump and found Slim asleep, tucked back against the wall where no one could see him.

"Make him a blanket from the bubbles." Maggie looked at him, curled tight in a ball. "Do it."

"You're super bossy." Bernie held out his hands and made his mouth into the shape of an 'o', leaning forward on his toes as he pushed out softball sized bubbles that knit themselves together in a dark blue translucent blanket, falling gently onto Slim. They quickly changed into wool as Maggie reached down and covered his shoulder. "That's something."

"That's something your mother would have done."

"Maybe, if she wasn't eating one of her brownies."

"That's the kind of attitude that makes this magic tough to do."

"Then, how come you get anything done?"

"Well played, sister. Are we done now? Let's get outta

here while we can." Bernie rubbed his hands together, speeding up until they were a blur. Just as suddenly, he pulled them apart, creating a large, oversized translucent bubble that encased them both. "Hang on," he said, grabbing onto her arm. "We can take this one together."

CHAPTER THIRTEEN

The large bubble quietly popped, leaving them in a dark parking lot. Maggie looked around and realized they were on the west side of the city.

They were standing outside the Galaxy Cafe that was doing a bustling business for dinner. "See anyone you recognize?"

Maggie leaned forward from where they stood in the dark in the parking lot between two pickup trucks, staring at the distant window. "Not from where we're standing."

"This is where the compass was not too long ago." Bernie held the sextant up to the stars, reading the numbers that floated out from it, disappearing just as soon as they appeared.

"How old is that thing?"

"It's called a sextant and it's older than this ship. We brought it with us on the journey when we set out on this trip. A three-hour tour." He looked at Maggie's surprise. "I'm kidding, kid. Don't you ever watch TV? Geez, what are they teaching you guys these days? Some good stuff on there. Those Golden Girls, they crack me up."

"You get distracted easily."

"Not really. I know why we're here. I can multi-task, it's a finer point of being a Huldu, especially when you have to keep such a large ship functioning as well as it can. I know we've had our moments but come on. This trip has lasted thousands of years past its arrival time."

"Every time you tell me something it gives me ten more questions to ask, like where are we really from?"

"Peabrains? You're from another galaxy." Bernie waved his hand absentmindedly in the air, pointing in a due south direction. "Nice area, lots of places to visit. This was more of a long-distance trek that would have taken a dozen years. Hence, the big ship, top of the line and newest model back then. We were only supposed to be passing through the Milky Way. Not too many like to stop here. Too many of the destinations are inhospitable."

"Until you took that wrong turn."

"Don't you start. There are plenty of mechanics who still like to talk about that little error in judgment."

Maggie looked up at the night sky. "There are more of us out there somewhere."

"Sure, as long as giant space worms or some kind of war or a weird virus didn't get them all. Oh, this is the part where I give you hope. Sorry, really new to this mentor thing. I'm trying here," he said, waving his hands."

It was useful when the Earth was actually moving through the cosmos." He held it up for her to look at it. "It was linked to the inner workings of the machinery."

"The parts you scattered all over the world."

"Not necessarily. Frankly, no one has known who the Elementals are for hundreds of years. You're the first we've discovered in a very long time. There could be two in one town and no one would know it. This sextant is what helped me locate the compass in your garage. I tried for years but no signal. Then, for some reason the thing lit up a few days ago and started spitting out data again."

"What did Jack say about it?"

Bernie looked sheepish, glancing up at the stars. "I didn't tell him. I know I should have but I wasn't sure what he would do with it. The mechanics want to go home," he said wistfully. He looked back at Maggie. "I'm not sure where home is anymore." He looked around at the quiet houses not far away. "Who's to say a ship can't be home? Works for Star Trek."

"That's not real and you watch too much TV."

"Details. But it's still the same. This place has grown on me."

"I'm going inside. We're not going to learn anything lurking out here."

"Hey, I thought we were sharing. What, no hug?"

"I'll hug you after we find the compass." Maggie strode up to the door and went inside, blinking at the lights. She grabbed a menu from a wooden holder by the door and glanced at it for a moment, looking up to scan the room.

Bernie was right behind her, eagerly taking a menu and walking toward the cashier at the other end of the room. A musty odor of overturned soil followed him.

"Hey, we're not here to eat. It's only 5:30." Maggie tried keeping her voice low, smiling at the surprised waiter passing by. "Looking for a friend. Might stay and eat, you never know," she muttered. She tried smiling and giving him a nod as he raised his eyebrows but kept walking.

Bernie looked back, rolling his eyes and turned, still heading for the counter. Maggie pressed her lips together and took another look around. She followed Bernie, still holding tight to the menu. "Stop walking, I have a date later. I can't take time to eat."

Bernie ignored her and smiled at the cashier and pointed to the menu. "I'll take the Zocala Buddha bowl and throw some steak on top of there."

Maggie came and stood next to him, still holding the menu. "That's probably the healthiest you've eaten in a while."

"What can I say? You have to adapt. It has cheese, meat, corn and tortilla chips in it. I'll eat around the beans. Order something, we may be here for some time and I'm hungry." He leaned closer to her and whispered, "You don't want to see a gnome when they're too hungry."

Maggie stared back at him and he held her gaze not blinking. "Fine," she said, holding up the menu. "I'll take the same."

"She's paying," said Bernie, grabbing the rolled-up silverware and empty water glass. He wandered off to find a table without looking back.

"Of course I am." Maggie paid the bill and found Bernie sitting by the window at a small table.

"Best view of the room," he said, hitching his thumb at the window. "And we can see who's coming and going in the parking lot. The sextant seems to feel pretty good about this place. The compass was here for a little while."

"That could be as simple as someone stopping to eat for a while before moving on, never to return."

"Very true, and if you have a better idea for us to pursue, please speak up. No? Okay, then we sit here, eat something and see what the universe dishes up. Worst case, we aren't running on empty. Best case, we get another clue." He leaned forward and put his rough, wide hand on top of Maggie's. "We'll find the compass and we'll find it in time."

Maggie sat back, letting her hand rest under his. "I believe we will, I do, but no one's going to make it easy."

"Well, that's a given. Oooh, food, at last."

The waitress put the food down in front of them and Bernie picked the large bowl up in his hands, holding it close to his face, grunting and snorting as he ate.

"Okay, I guess we can take a short break for food. But I have a date in a couple of hours. Eat fast."

CHAPTER FOURTEEN

Simon Wesley sat behind his desk in his office with the door closed. On his lap sat open an ancient book bound in leather with page after page of hieroglyphics. In his hand sat the compass, the five small black arms frozen in position.

He rubbed his temples, feeling the beginning of a headache and swallowed hard. "Ten years studying this thing, day and night and still the details get away from me," he hissed, clenching his teeth in anger. His chest heaved up and down with each breath as he did his best to calm down. He ran his finger over each symbol, repeating each phrase. "One for each element of the earth, but the compass is the key."

He poked the last symbol. It had always bothered him, never feeling quite right. "The compass is the key." His eyes widened in surprise, even delight as a flood of relief came over him. "Not compass, not compass at all. The Elemental who holds the compass." His relief quickly turned to a million thoughts racing through his mind. "The Elemental is the only one who can use the compass. Maggie Parker has to be willing to hold the compass and use it as a guide. Willing." A chill went down his spine. "It's necessary, if only she knew. We have to travel back to where we came from and return home, at last. But first I have to get her to come to me."

He got up and went over to one of his examining trays, holding up the compass under a lit, oversized magnifying glass. "You hold the key to everyone's future, Maggie Parker. You and this ancient piece of metal that has traveled through the stars. There's got to be a way to convince you I'm right." His eyes flashed a deep blood red for a moment, leaving him with a faint ache at the back of his neck.

He picked up his phone and sent out a group text. *Meet me at the old location.* He sent out a separate text to one of his longest followers, Raymond Twiller. He had believed in Simon's story from the beginning. He was one of the few people Simon trusted.

Follow her and don't take your eyes off her. Let me know if you see anything suspicious.

Simon drove around the back of the old warehouse on the outskirts of Austin on the southeast side. It was a peculiar thing about the bustling city that just miles away were open stretches of land and old warehouses of failed businesses. Simon was familiar with this particular one because it had been the scene of a gruesome double homicide. The land had sat vacant ever since and locals still avoided it. It was the perfect meeting place.

They were already there waiting for him, huddled near the back wall of the metal building, standing out of the cold. Simon parked his car and got out carrying a satchel. He walked toward the padlock he had put on the door to keep neighborhood kids out. The owner's widow had moved to Boca years ago and abandoned the property, wanting nothing more to do with it. No one noticed he had taken it over.

He brushed his silver bangs out of his eyes, unlocked the padlock, opened the wide door and went inside, pushing past the dusty large boxes that had '48 Tools in One' printed on the side in bright red letters. He went to the center of the ware-house and fired up the generator, making his way around the room, turning on a lamp and checking for any signs of vagrants. Nothing was disturbed. The wards he had placed around the property were working. He stifled a yawn, keeping his back to the crowd of twenty people keeping a respectful distance just outside the pool of light from the lamp.

Simon appreciated the show of respect, even expected it. After all, he held the key to the human beings' deliver-ance, if only everyone would listen.

He smiled, his eyes still a cold, flat blue. "We are making progress on the grand operation."

There was a murmur of voices and everyone looked around as Simon patiently raised his hand to quiet them down. He had waited so long for this moment, he wasn't going to lose his temper and spoil it. "We have the compass..."

Again, he had to raise his hand for quiet, but he understood. He felt the same thrill run through him at the mention of their success. "It's all thanks to Brother Frank Winters service."

The thin, neatly dressed man gave a slight bow, brushing down his beard. His arm was tucked in a sling.

"But it turns out that is only half the battle. The compass is lifeless without its true owner, the Elemental, Maggie Parker. Without her, this great ship…" He held up his arms dramatically, stretching them out wide, "that we call Mother Earth is rudderless. We cannot go anywhere. Now, to a lot of people that would sound like the ideal solution. Stay with what we know! But we know better. There's another place for us out among the stars in an entirely different galaxy." He rubbed his hands together, pulling them apart to reveal an oversized bubble that grew to fill the space between them full of a distant constellation no one in their generation had ever seen. The followers ooohed and aaaaahed, their eyes opening wider.

"A paradise that is ours to return to and family lines that will welcome us back, if we could only get there."

"We need to grab Maggie Parker!" An older woman with wiry gray hair dressed in tight brown pants and a short navy-blue jacket shouted from the back. "Make her do it!"

Simon smiled patiently. "That, unfortunately will not work, and besides, we know in the end it's not necessary. We have the story, the evidence to show her." He was practically shouting, his face flushed. He went to the satchel propped up against an empty blue storage bin and opened it, pulling out the old book. "This ancient diary tells our story." He held it up gingerly, gently shaking it. "We come from nirvana where there were no wars, no famine, no floods. Of course things have gone wrong here! We're on an organic ship that was never designed to be a permanent home." His voice broke at the end and he had to take a deep breath and pause for a moment.

"We are the ones who have woken up and know that magic is real and human beings possess so much more inside themselves. We can show Maggie Parker what and who we really are as a group! We are all the evidence she needs."

He held out his hands and blew into them, his eyes briefly flashing a deep red. No one noticed. They were too focused on his hands. Large opaque bubbles formed instantly and joined together, forming one, even larger bubble. "I've been working on a little something to deal with her protectors so we can get closer to Ms. Parker. Damn Huldus would ship us off to a place unknown! They are a threat to our very existence and a roadblock to our happiness. Join me with your energy!"

Simon's followers put their hands into the circle, the bubbles all joining together, twisting and turning toward the ceiling. Ropey vines appeared inside the massive bubble and large, flat leaves unfurled, exposing a deep violet blossom with a sweet perfume. The bubbles surrounding the vines slid off, forming a foam at the base that sizzled and popped. A follower reached out and touched a blossom, yelping in pain, even as Simon lunged forward to stop him. The man's skin was already bubbling and oozing, dotted with small razor-sharp thorns.

The vines bent toward the man, reaching out their

vines and he ran for the door. Simon opened his arms wide, setting a new intention but it wasn't working. The vines scurried after the follower, catching him around the ankles and dragging him back. The others pressed back, jumping into the shadows as Simon worked furiously, waving his arms around and mumbling every spell he could remember from the ancient diary. Black splotches appeared on the vine opening up steam vents and an acrid smell that burned the eyes, but the vines were determined.

A tentacle peeled away, swiping Simon across the chest, sending him crashing to the floor, a burn mark across his jacket.

There was a tearing sound as the vines created an opening in the center, pulling the captured follower inside even as he screamed, and the other followers looked on in horror. Even the older woman who had shaken her fist earlier had her hands pressed against her mouth. The man disappeared into the center of the vines as they closed around him, muffling his screams till the room became silent once again.

"That was a very mixed success." Simon stood up, shaken, and brushed off his pants. He pressed his lips together in a thin line and pulled the front of his singed jacket away from his body not looking at anyone. He cleared his throat and lifted his chin. "No one wants to see a good man sacrifice himself like that." He cleared his throat again. "Let's make sure it wasn't in vain. Everyone needs to keep their wits about them and realize this isn't a game." His voice was low, but he spit out the last words. "Give this mission the respect it deserves." He did his best to stand up straighter and adjust his clothing the best he could as he made his way around the vine.

He startled, a slight tremor passing through him as he came to where the opening had been and saw the outline of a face, twisted into a scream.

CHAPTER FIFTEEN

Maggie stood in the West Austin Neighborhood Park away from the street lights. "We look like we're up to no good."

"It was your idea to come to a park just down the street from your house. I think I can see the smoke rising up from your mom's place from here. That crowd loves their funny cigarettes." Bernie held out his hands. "No judgment, of course."

"Of course. I'm told it's medicinal."

"Of course. Now focus, it's time you learned how to control some of this magic. It'll come in handy if you get cornered by a Kashgar. Those tall bastards."

"I'm trying."

"To quote a rather famous distant cousin of mine. There is no try. There is only do."

"That's not the quote."

"Close enough, now come on, shake off what happened at the Galaxy Cafe, or what didn't happen. If we stare at what we don't have for too long, we'll miss the really small clues that add up to locating the compass. You ready?"

"Ready as I'll ever be." She looked down at her phone. "I only have an hour."

"I know, you have a date. Only trying to save your life here."

"I'm not the best at this whole dating thing. I can't afford to ghost this guy. He seems normal. That's harder to find than you think."

"That's crazy. You're young, hot and pay your own bills. Has to be a dozen guys who'd buy that."

"I'm told I don't come off as warm and inviting."

"Nooooo, you? I'm sorry but making you trusting is third level magic. Let's just stick with something easy tonight."

"Hardy har har. Less than an hour and then I have to go. I need the practice at that too." Maggie took a deep breath and felt the cold air fill her nose and go into her lungs. She always like this time of year. Her leather jacket was just warm enough against the wind.

She looked around, making herself take in the shadows as the trees blew in the wind and felt the cushion of the grass underneath her feet. The moon was only half full, illuminating the stars but covering most of the ground in darkness. "It's a beautiful night," she whispered.

"When you're ready, put out your hand and concentrate on creating bubbles of light. Nothing too hotshot. It can have just a glow and we'll call it a victory."

Maggie felt the soft spread of a tingle on the back of her neck and a crooked smile spread across her face. She felt a mild ringing in her ears as she held out both hands, palms up and opened her mouth. A cool thread of magic spread through her mind as a bubble grew just inside her mouth, glowing through her cheeks. The smell of magnolias filled her nostrils.

It slipped effortlessly out of her mouth and rose into a nearby redbud tree, resting on a branch before popping, the light disappearing in a twinkle.

"Bravo! You have accomplished a basic bubble and nothing's on fire. Okay, do it again." Bernie was smiling from ear to ear, his thumbs underneath his overalls.

"What's with the smell whenever there's magical bubbles?"

"It's like a fingerprint. Everyone has their own variety." Bernie hesitated, clearing his throat.

"Don't do that." Maggie pursed her lips in annoyance.

"Do what?"

"Tell me half of something. What's the other part?"

"It's not good that you can already see my tells."

Maggie put her hands on his shoulders with a firm grip. "Spill."

"Fine, there are exceptions. None of them good. Those who dabble in dark magic, their bubbles rot. The scent starts out all right and pleasant, but it quickly stinks to high heaven. Like rotten eggs." He let out a sigh and shrugged. "Might as well tell you the other one. Sometimes, we have found that a Peabrain can join forces with other Peabrains and merge their magic. The scent becomes the trademark tell of the leader of the pack. Also bad news. That much magic tends to warp the head guy because your little average peabrain wasn't designed to hold that much power. They start to burn out. Poor decision making of the evil kind generally follows. Now, come on, enough chitchat. Focus, do another bubble."

"You weren't worried I could do it at all, were you, Bernie?"

"Not at all. You're an Elemental."

"What happened to rule number four?"

"That's not a lie. I knew you'd get there eventually. Go on, do another. Try for a string of them. All you have to do is imagine it and then, let the peabrain part of you do the rest. Surrender to it."

"Surrender to it," Maggie whispered. "Become the observer."

"Never said that but okay, sure if that works for you."

The chatter coming from Bernie faded into the background and Maggie listened for the other noises across the park. She heard rustling in the bushes nearby and wondered if it was the McCreary's cat out for an evening stroll. She heard a car honk in the distance and pictured people still coming out of the bars on Fifth Street. The cool thread spread out across her brain, filling her head and she felt a sense of calm fill her chest. She opened her mouth to exclaim and was surprised to see a string of bubbles emerge, all of them glowing from the inside, tied together like twinkle lights, one right after the other. *Breathe, keep breathing.*

The bubbles floated on the wind, swirling through the trees, wrapping themselves around the branches of an old live oak that spread its branches across a corner of the park.

Maggie went to stand beneath it, keeping her mouth open for as long as she could till her jaw began to ache and the branches had taken on their own glow. "It's beautiful," she said, cutting off the stream of bubbles. The lights held in the tree, twinkling against the leaves.

"Not bad, Maggie Parker," said Bernie, softly, his head back, smiling at the light. It cast a gentle yellow glow all around the knobby roots just underneath. "The bubbles are holding their shape. That's a good sign. You have a lot of promise. The Elemental indeed." Reluctantly, he waved his hand and a stream of gold sparks shot out, quickly finding their mark and popping all the bubbles, putting out the light.

Maggie snapped her mouth shut and felt the calm leave again. "I suppose an unusual beacon of light right near my house would attract the wrong kind of attention."

"Yeah, but it's probably made your mother's night."

Maggie let out a laugh and patted Bernie on his shoulder. "I'll bet they drum about it for days. I wish I could tell Diana everything. She deserves to know, doesn't she?"

"Deserves, definitely, but you'll put her at risk. Now, come on, we're not done. Those bubbles were pretty, but they were child's play. You need to keep going. Someday you'll tell her everything. This time, I want you to try to create something small inside a bubble. Something easy, please. Nothing with a beating heart." Bernie shivered, his eyes widening. "Man, that is never a good idea when you're starting out. I've seen some creations, hoo boy!"

"Got it, I'm convinced. I'll think of something easy." An image of toothpicks popped into her head and wouldn't leave. She held onto it and felt the icy chill that was already becoming familiar leaving her a little light headed. She leaned against the old oak and yelped with surprise. Her hand easily slipped through the bark and inside the tree. She took a step back, pulling her hand almost all the way out, just as her heel struck a root, tripping her forward, into the tree.

The world went dark for a moment and Maggie could feel the warmth of her breath bouncing off something nearby. But just as suddenly, a pale blue glow erupted inside of the tree, lighting all of the pathways up and down the trunk, illuminating the insects crawling furiously for the top. She could hear Bernie's muffled shouting, barely making out the words.

"Are you okay? Boy, this is a new one!" Bernie stood on the outside, slapping the tree with one hand, while patting the top of his head in frustration. "Is there even air in there? Can you hear me? Think, Bernie, think. What kind of bubbles do I use for this? Jack is never going to let me forget this!"

Maggie put out her hand and a trail of glowing, pale blue ladybugs jumped on to her arm, crawling up to her hand. She lifted her hand and let them crawl back onto the tree. "How is this possible?" The light swirled around her taking up all the space but leaving room for her at the same time. She could feel the vibrations of the tree pulsing through her and down into the roots. The tree was receiving messages from other trees and sending just as quickly in a continuous pattern that streamed back and forth.

She could hear the messages in her head, overlapping each other one right after the other.

"You are always talking," she said with delight, turning in a tight circle, the blue glow reflecting in her eyes. She held up her hands to her face, feeling the vibration pass through her cheeks as the bubbles poured out of her mouth, even as she giggled and laughed. Small, jeweled beetles appeared in some of the bubbles, while others held tiny butterflies that spread their wings as the bubbles popped and flew just above Maggie's head in a circle, creating an iridescent crown above her head.

Bernie circled the tree on the outside, wringing his hands, still occasionally knocking against the wood, yelling as loudly as he dared, the words whistling through his teeth. He didn't want to attract the neighbors or alert any mechanics who might be checking the gauges underneath the ground and hear a Huldu in distress. That would bring a small squadron running. "No, no, not just yet. Might be able to fix it. Maggie! You okay? Still breathing, I hope." Sweat ran down the side of his face and he licked his dry lips, feeling his heart pound in his chest. "Wooo boy, this is a pickle."

A connection to the trees, a hum of energy, ran straight through Maggie, filling her with a kind of joy she had not known for a long time. She was rooted to something in this world, a kinship.

Her forehead wrinkled and her eyes widened in surprise as she realized what the trees were buzzing about.

"Maggie, let me know something! Knock twice if you can hear me! What am I saying? Knock at all, I'll assume it's you."

Maggie startled out of her reverie and put out her hands trying to grab onto the glowing light and keep the feeling. "No, not yet!" She put out her hands to touch the inner veins of the tree and felt herself fall through, coming out the other side into a forward roll across the roots. "Ooof," flew out of her mouth and the wind knocked out of her lungs, leaving her lying on her back for a moment looking up at the stars. The feeling was gone, but the memory was still there. She wanted to hold onto it for just a moment longer.

Bernie came running around the tree, almost tripping over her and stopping just at her feet. "You're here! You went through an entire tree! You're still in one piece!" He spluttered, spitting out small bubbles and fireflies in a rapid succession, clapping his hands together.

A porch light went on across the street and Bernie clapped a hand across his mouth to stop the stream of tiny flickering lights from attracting a good hard look. A woman on the ground with a stout old man standing over her was not going to end well for him. "This is good news," he finally whispered, his heart still pounding. He put a hand to his chest, swallowing hard. "You went through a frickin' tree!"

Maggie sat up on her elbows and felt the beginning of a mild headache. "I think I have tree hangover. You've gone through the ground thousands of times, I imagine. What's so special about going through one tree?"

"Trees are different, always have been. It's in our manual we keep in the engine room. They don't let anything bigger than a bug move through them. Something about disrupting the daisy chain they've got going on for themselves. No one has ever seen the inside of a tree!" Bernie bent over and put his hands on his knees, taking in steady, even breaths. "This screw up would have been right up there with that wrong turn around the meteor shower. I wouldn't even know how to explain it! There was no proof left behind."

"I'm fine, thank you." Maggie got herself up to a standing position and cautiously leaned against the tree, still hoping to feel something. A small vibration passed through her and a small smile came across her lips. *It's still talking.*

"You were a Keebler elf there for a few minutes." Bernie pulled an old handkerchief out of his pocket and wiped the sweat off his face.

"We're going to get the compass back." Maggie felt her head clearing and stood up straighter, her hands on her hips.

"I know, I'm the one who's been telling you."

"No, I mean I know we are. The trees are helping. They're all looking for the compass and relaying what they find." Her eyes shined in the darkness. "A million trees are keeping watch."

"Very kumbaya and everything, but whoever has it may not be dangling it outside. Don't get me wrong. Okay, okay." Bernie threw up his hands. "This is why I don't get invited to too many parties. Makes me uncomfortable when things get too touchy-feely. I like a little sand in everything."

"Some have said the same about me." Maggie started walking down Pressler in the direction of her house.

"You don't say?" Bernie followed behind her, blowing bubbles that caught the moonlight and twinkled like little stars following behind them.

"Oh crap, I have to go. The hour's almost up and I can't go looking like this." Maggie took off running down the street, easily outpacing Bernie, who ran behind her for a block, flapping his arms to get her attention. She was gone without turning back to look at him.

"That girl needs more than a date." The gnome walked back to the park and found a place on the grass. He took a quick look around to make sure the coast was clear and waved his arm, disappearing from view.

Raymond Twiller stepped out of the shadows after everyone was gone and sent a text to Simon that all was well. Then, he turned and ran down the street past the large three-story stucco, toward the Caribbean blue bungalow not far from the corner. He circled around the corner and came down the alley behind the bungalow and in through the back gate passing by the garage. The chickens were already roosting in their coop for the night and didn't hear him pass them by. He planted himself just far enough away to be able to see all the windows. He was planning to settle in for the night.

"You want to tell me what you're doing following me?" Maggie tapped him hard on the shoulder and shoved him for good measure.

Raymond spun around, a surprised comical look on his face, his arms starting to raise. Maggie saw the pattern of four small stars in a random pattern just inside his wrist. She didn't hesitate.

He never saw the fist coming.

"I'm never gonna make this date," she muttered, pulling out her phone.

Diana came through the house, racing down the back steps, her red wavy hair loose around her face. Her usual calm demeanor was gone. She grabbed Maggie by the shoulders, quickly looking her over and shooting questions at her. "Are you okay? Did he hurt you? What did he say? Do we know the creep?"

"Diana, I'm good. Remember what I do for a living. I took him out."

Her sister was already checking on Raymond, crouching next to him. "He's already coming to. You got him good in the chin. Nicely done, sister."

Maggie came down to her sister's level and whispered. "Diana, do you think you can help me get him out of here without anyone seeing us?"

Diana gave her sister a hard look. "I'm Toni Parker's daughter, this sort of thing is definitely in my wheelhouse. Come on, I'll get his feet."

"Mom has taken us on a few adventures. Remember the time she left us at the movies when we were in elementary school?" She could barely see Diana's face in the darkness.

"Yeah, and it turned out to be a triple horror feature starring Vincent Price. Didn't come back for hours. I also remember I waited in the lobby, but you refused to wait with me."

"It was the only movies we were going to get for the foreseeable future, and I gave you my Raisinettes."

"You've always been fearless." Diana stood up, looking around to see if anyone was out walking their dog.

"Out of necessity. It's not quite the same thing as

courage. Aren't you going to ask me where we're taking him? Or why I'm not calling it in?"

"I trust you. Now, come on, let's get a move on. You have that date."

Maggie bent down and cradled Raymond's head and shoulders in her arms. "Lift with your knees, not your back. You really think I can still make a date?"

"It's the fourth date! You normally don't get this far. If I have to carry this guy myself, you're gonna make that date."

They stood up, dangling Raymond between them, his butt skimming along the ground. "Where *are* we taking him?" asked Diana. "Your car is out front."

"The garage for now. He can sleep it off in there. You still know how to do that knot we learned in rodeo camp?"

"You mean the wrap and cinch double column? Probably? Hell, I'll figure it out."

"You're a really good big sister. Are you dressed in pajama bottoms?"

Diana grunted as they inched their way around to the side door of the garage. "Hey, I was off work. Don't judge while we're carrying a man knocked out by your fist."

They dropped Raymond Twiller in a corner of the garage near the bags of chicken feed and trussed his hands and feet, securing him to a metal pipe and taping duct tape over his mouth.

"Should I ask who he is?" Diana stood back and looked at their handiwork. "No way he's even moving from where he is."

"He's part of a bigger mystery. I can stay and tell you all about it or…"

Diana took Maggie by the shoulders. "This day started

with a robbery in here. Something good should happen today! This guy can wait till you get back, I'll make sure of it. Go on that date!"

Maggie hugged her sister. "I promise I'll tell you everything, later."

"Goes without saying, now go get ready." Diana tried to smile at her sister but settled for squeezing her hand, leaving Maggie with the distinct impression she knew more than she was telling. But she was already pushing Maggie out of the garage and toward the house. Any stories about gnomes or questions about Elementals would have to wait till later.

CHAPTER SIXTEEN

Maggie let the rideshare drop her off at the corner. She saw Jake from a block away standing nervously outside of Swift's Attic Restaurant on Congress Avenue. She had hastily taken a shower and pulled on her favorite blue dress, wincing at the purple and black bruise blooming along her ribs as she pulled the dress over her head.

She crossed the street and waved as he noticed her, a smile instantly coming across his face, surprising her.

"Hey, you haven't been waiting long?" She stepped up onto the curb, and he covered the short distance between them, kissing her briefly on the lips, his hand on her elbow.

Maggie turned in time to see an elderly man patiently waiting by the curb nearby for his wife, smiling at her with his hand out. "Beautifully done, dear," he said, kissing his wife's hand as she let out a delighted laugh and wove her hand inside his offered arm. They turned and headed down the side street as Maggie watched for a moment, mesmerized. *That's what I want.*

Jake followed her gaze and smiled, offering his arm to Maggie. She felt her face redden and pressed her lips together, even as she took his arm and felt a small thrill as her fingers wrapped around his strong bicep. She looked up at him and smiled. *I can do this.*

Her confidence rose and she imagined just how she'd tell Diana she rocked this fourth date. Not such an unsolvable mystery after all. Of course, that was just before she felt the toe of her shoe make solid contact with the uneven sidewalk. It was too late.

Her forward momentum carried her toward the ground, even as she held tight to Jake's arm. Her purse went flying through the air, the strap slipping off her shoulder and the contents spraying across the sidewalk. The Austin gold shield came to rest right next to her favorite carnation red lipstick.

Jake quickly pivoted, blocking her from falling all the way to her knees, but providing a perfect place for her to mash her face into his neatly pressed white shirt. She let out an "Oof," feeling a short current of pain from her ribs. She gritted her teeth for a moment, determined to ignore it. She was already making enough of a scene.

"Are you okay?" His look of concern was only making it worse. She glanced back and forth between his face and the perfect red carnation lip imprint on the center of his shirt.

"I am so sorry." Maggie reached out and touched his chest, only to realize she was touching his chest and yanked her hand back, her eyes widening. "Hang on, I've got this." She crouched down in her best heels, tucking her dress as she reached out and scooped her belongings toward her. Jake knelt down beside her, handing her the badge as she pulled out a tissue and dabbed at the lipstick stain, leaving an even larger smear. "Oh… no…"

She finally looked back at his face, crouched next to him there on the sidewalk and realized he was grinning from ear to ear. "It's okay. Maybe I can get you to autograph it later and I can keep it as a memento."

Maggie's mouth dropped open, trying to think of something to say, but instead laughter bubbled up, spilling out. Jake's smile spread to his eyes, lines deepening around them as he held out his hand and helped her stand up.

Maggie kept on laughing, Jake's arm around her back as she scanned the sidewalk for anything else.

Jake placed her hand back inside the crook of his arm. "That was really nice of you to break the ice for both of us tonight. Very generous. Things can only get easier from here."

Maggie let out a giggle and they walked the rest of the way to the restaurant. "I can't guarantee that, Jake. It's been a really weird day and we have a few hours ahead of us. I'd suggest you just keep that bar low."

He held open the door. "Sounds like we already have our first topic of discussion."

The smile left Maggie's face for a moment. How would she talk about any of it? "Work's not my favorite topic. Or my mother, or my father." She was talking way too fast.

"We all have complicated families. After you?" He pointed to the stairs that led up to the restaurant on the second floor.

"Best to leave my family out of it altogether. How about those Cowboys?" The general sense of impending doom she usually got when on a date was creeping back inside of her.

She marched up the long flight of stairs, making faces that Jake couldn't see, coming up the narrow stairs behind her. *I can outrun a perp. I am a good sister and a daughter. Apparently, I can now talk to trees...*

"Did you see they kept a good wide receiver with potential and a fullback who can block?"

Maggie jerked her head back to look over her shoulder and saw the same broad smile across Jake's face.

"Randall Cobb would make a good choice as a wide receiver," she said. All those hours of listening to Taylor talk endlessly about the Cowboys was about to pay off.

Jake's eyebrows went up and he tilted his head. "Ah, not bad, not bad at all. Better watch where you're going till we get to the top." He smiled again, even though Maggie was looking at the stain on his shirt as much as the grin on his face.

"Right, no more Cirque de Soleil moves for tonight."

"Well, I didn't say that…"

Maggie laughed as they reached the hostess, forgetting herself for a moment. "Yeah, I know, fourth date protocol…"

The hostess smiled, picking up two menus. "Right this way."

Maggie realized what she had said and sputtered, trying to think of something else to say. She was out of football quotes.

Jake slipped his arm back around her waist. "How about it's just a dinner date and we can get to know each other even better. We'll throw the protocol out and figure this out for ourselves."

He pulled out her chair and waited for her to take a seat as she felt herself take in a slow, deep breath. "Even better plan." She shook her head. "I kind of have this honesty thing that I can't shake. I say what I'm thinking a lot of the time and sometimes the most interesting things come out."

"I've noticed." He put up his hand in protest. "And I like it. Don't lose that. I like how direct you are. I never have to guess what you're thinking."

Maggie glanced down at the menu. "So, you're a manager at the CVS on Guadalupe. You haven't said much about it. What's that like?"

"Sometimes it's like herding cats and we always have to keep an extra storage space for the cash register tape."

"Oh, yeah, good one. I get it. ExtraBucks. Long… receipt…" Maggie held her hand up in the air. Jake made being on a date look so easy. It was helping.

"We're known for that and our 'as seen on TV' aisle. That's where I generally do all my gift shopping."

"Good to know. Practical and economical. You can even get a discount."

"My mother says I'm always thinking. Have you been here before? The Korean shrimp and grits are really good."

"That's the first time I've heard you mention your family."

"They're an interesting bunch. Loud and opinionated and a lot of cousins."

Maggie sat back and listened to him talk, her shoulder dropping as she gave a small smile. *He is so easy to be with.*

Dinner progressed without knocking over a wine glass or a lull in the conversation. Maggie found herself telling Jake about Diana, and the time their father took them to Barton Springs pool but told them to stay away from the deep end. "Of course, I didn't listen and dove in feet first and immediately sank like a rock. Diana jumped in after me and pulled me to the side before Dad found out. I was so thankful to her I gave her one of my best Barbies. But then she confessed and spilled that I ruined her cannonball and she pulled me out of there because I was in the way."

"Oooh, so both of you have to be honest." Jake laughed, taking a sip of his wine.

"Looks that way, even though Diana swears with me it's chronic."

A trill sounded and Jake scrambled for his phone. "Sorry, thought I had muted it. Hey, it's the store, hang on just a moment."

"A CVS emergency? Sure, no problem."

Jake gave a tight smile, holding the phone up to his ear.

Maggie wrinkled her forehead and looked around the restaurant, trying not to eavesdrop. Jake held up a finger and slowly rose from his chair.

"I'll only be a minute, I promise."

"No problem," nodded Maggie. "Must be out of register tape," she muttered as he walked toward the men's room. She checked her own phone. Only a text from her sister reminding her to wear the good underwear. "What, did I think a gnome who lives under the ground would text me?"

She sat back, picking up her wine glass and took a healthy sip. "Yeah, one weird day."

"Why are you calling me? I thought I made myself clear." Jake hissed into the phone, huddling near the kitchen. He glanced around the corner at Maggie pouring herself a healthy fill from the wine bottle and ducked back before she turned her head in his direction.

"I know what the mission is, and I understand my duty. But, like I've already said more than once, I'm also half human, not just Kashgar. Besides, you haven't shown me any proof that she's that valuable to some cause." He ran his hand through his hair, the frustration building.

"Yes, some cause." He said it louder than he intended, and the sous chef looked up from the carrots he was chopping, glancing over at Jake.

"You tell me a bunch of stories that are supposed to be thousands of years old and some grand scheme and I'm supposed to just buy it because you said it. So, yeah, *some* cause." He shook his head. "It's not enough to get me to do what you're talking about. Not by a mile." He glanced nervously at his watch. "I'm going, I've been gone too long as it is. Do what you want, but I'm out."

The menacing voice of the local Kashgar leader on the other end spoke very clearly and very slowly. "You had better keep a close eye on her and report back, at the very least. And before you interrupt me again, keep in mind that if you don't, I'll send someone else and they may not be as enchanted by the Elemental as you are. As a matter of fact, maybe I should just take my own advice."

"Fine!" Jake cut him off. "I'll report back but that's all you'll get from me." He hung up the phone before the leader could say anything else and stood there, waiting for his heart rate to slow down, slowly counting to ten. He was going to have to find a way to tell them about Maggie Parker and the compass but without getting either one of them killed. "Or letting her find out about my complicated family."

Jake walked swiftly back to the table, making sure to plant a smile on his face. He slid into his seat and looked over at Maggie.

"Everything okay?" she asked.

"What? Oh, yeah, just some mix up with a delivery. The assistant manager wasn't sure what to say and they were pressing her for an answer."

"You ever notice how a CVS Pharmacy and a Walgreen's are always close to each other? And they're everywhere." Maggie giggled, letting out a burp, slapping her hand over her mouth. She could feel the effects of the wine. "Well, you did say you like how transparent I am," she said through her fingers.

Jake smiled and reached across the table for her other hand, holding it tight. "Let's take a walk under the stars."

Maggie looked at him, startled, glancing at his wrists. No tattoo. *Okay, let it go. This is Jake and this is the fourth date.*

Jake insisted on driving Maggie home and walking her all the way to her door. Her buzz from the wine had worn off and she was left with trying to enjoy the moment while pushing out thoughts about the strange man with the star tattoo trussed up in her garage and if Diana was watching out of any of the windows. She opened her mouth to say something just as Jake leaned in and gently opened his mouth, licking the edge of her teeth. She felt her shoulders relax and just for a moment, she forgot about the very weird day.

She wrapped her arms around him and met his tongue with her own. Magic and talking trees and mystery thugs in the garage would have to wait a minute or two. *Maybe I do know how to do this.*

She felt his hand slide across the small of her back and pull her closer, her chin tilted up. *Yeah, this is nice. Sure, I could do second base. Why not, I'm a grown up. Is that what they still call it? Of course it is...*

Jake tenderly bit her bottom lip and slid his tongue back in, pressing her closer.

Oh yeah... Okay... Never mind. At last, the thoughts stopped spinning around in her head.

The grackles sitting on the electric lines above let out a squawk, taking flight. There was a message to deliver, the Elemental had returned home safely. The Huldus would want to know.

Maggie heard them in the background but failed to notice anything unusual. She was a little busy.

CHAPTER SEVENTEEN

Maggie stood in the doorway of her garage swearing under her breath. "Son of a..." The garage was empty and all that remained where there should have been a strange man were torn ropes. Diana's knot didn't hold. "I don't believe that. He didn't wriggle his way out of here. That's not what did it." Maggie had first-hand knowledge of getting hogtied by her sister when they were younger. Diana found her reading her diary and had chased her throughout the house and out to the backyard.

She had to promise a Barbie outfit and giving her cover with Mom when she snuck out to get Diana to untie her. The girls had started sneaking out at night at a young age and Maggie would have covered for her anyway.

"This guy has friends." Maggie crouched down, still in her heels and gently dug around the area, examining the rope ends. Clean cut, in strategic spots. "Whoever it was came prepared and knew what they were doing."

Just moments before she had been walking through the backyard, lightheaded, thinking about the feeling of kissing a man. Kissing Jake. But then she saw that the door was ajar, and she was immediately ripped back into the present circumstances of her life.

Magic, check. Planet really a ship, check. Same big world not happy she still exists, check. Compass, nope. Thug with strange tattoo tied up in the garage, also nope.

She had just been on her front porch wrapped in Jake's embrace for what felt like a moment but really lasted minutes. But then the porch light came on followed by the sound of Diana swearing and turning it back off just as quickly, interrupting the mood. They had sheepishly pulled apart with one last lingering kiss and a promise from Jake to wait at least till tomorrow before texting.

Maggie was still smiling when she passed by Diana who was standing by the kitchen island, apologizing profusely. Didn't matter. Maggie felt a warm thrill inside that had nothing to do with the back of her neck. A different kind of magic.

That was shoved aside, and a calm came over her as she easily slid into detachment and what had become instinct as a detective. She stood back up, hands on hips and assessed the scene, stepping back outside the garage to look up and down the alley, listening for any unusual sounds. There was nothing but the sound of traffic blocks away on Fifth Street. But to the left Maggie saw a small piece of the rope that had been left behind and went to retrieve it. The ends were driven over.

"He was picked up in a car." Hardly anything but trash trucks ever came down the alley. Not much of a clue but something to file away for later, just in case.

She let out a yawn and trudged back to the garage, securing the door once again. "This is becoming a habit."

Diana was coming down the steps toward her as she made her way to the house. "How's the guest?" asked Diana.

"MIA." Maggie held up the bits of rope. "I think he had help."

"What? No! I didn't hear a thing and I checked on him a half hour ago. He was still out cold. I even checked his eyes and his pulse. I don't think he was playing possum." Diana put her hand to her forehead, standing still on the steps.

Maggie stepped up, putting her hand on Diana's arm. "Hey, it's not your fault, you know. It looks like he had a buddy. I'm glad you didn't hear anything." Maggie suddenly felt a chill and hugged her sister tight.

"Hey, hey! What's this about? We're not the hugging type." Diana started walking back toward the garage, peeling her way out of Maggie's embrace. "What aren't you telling me? There's something gross back there, I can tell. You know I've cut up cadavers, put back together mangled hands, not to mention all the times I've cleaned up Mom's late nights."

Diana's red hair was pinned on top of her head and the light from the alley was casting a halo around her as she marched, determined and still talking. Maggie could tell she was angry.

"I'm not shielding you from anything. I know better than that. I wasn't calling you a wuss. Geez, come on back here. There's nothing to see." Maggie strode behind her, jogging a little in her high heels to catch up with her big sister. "You know I wouldn't keep you from something gross. You're my sister!"

Diana walked into the garage and spun around, looking in every direction, her eyes wide. She looked surprised as she turned and looked at Maggie standing back in the doorway. Her gaze narrowed and she crossed her arms over her chest. Maggie knew that look and took a deep breath. "That's your crap detector. There's no crap here and no body. He got away, that's it and I honestly don't know who he is or what he wanted." *A few good clues, sure. But I'm not telling you that I'm living on borrowed time and don't know how to fix it, yet. I love you too much for that bombshell.* "I'm going to figure this out, I promise." She made the Girl Scout salute and smiled. *I will figure this out.*

Diana uncrossed her arms but stood there with her hip out, thinking it over. "Don't keep me in the dark about it, okay?" She walked past Maggie out into the yard but turned around, her face brightening. "How was the date? A good one, I take it by the action on the front porch. Way to represent." She gave her little sister a playful punch in the arm and danced backward as Maggie swatted at her.

"It was nice, better than nice. I think I finally found a decent guy. Time will tell. Hey, you didn't eat all the Tiny Pies, did you? Love that place. Come on inside, I'll tell you all about it." She put her arm around her sister's shoulder and nudged them toward the house. "I only fell on my face once, but his chest caught me."

Diana let out a guffaw and looked at her sister, her eyes wide with delight. "No, really? Good thing his manliness was there to catch you. How'd he take it?"

"Just like you'd hope."

"Details," said Diana, holding open the door.

"Of course."

"Even the naughty parts."

"Of course, those are the best parts."

The morning sky was the standard blue for Austin weather and the locals idea of winter with the temperature dropping into the forties.

Maggie stood in her kitchen drinking her second cup of coffee. A mouse ran across the floor and stopped in front of her as if it wanted to say something. She paused, the mug halfway to her mouth and waited to see what would happen next. "I'm just gonna put down the coffee slowly and stand here." Her hands were already on her hips.

"You know, just a few days ago I would have gone to get a broom by now." She was looking directly at the mouse as it twitched its whiskers. "But today, I have to wonder if you could be a messenger, or a relative, or some key to saving the world." She picked the coffee back up and took a long sip, smiling at her own joke.

"Ah, coffee. Nectar of the gods. You want some?"

The mouse opened its tiny mouth as bubbles blew out and it rapidly changed into a short gnome she instantly recognized.

"Bernie! What the hell?" Maggie sloshed the coffee, jumping back before any of it could stain the front of her shirt. There wasn't enough time before work to change.

She had overslept, waking up with a dull headache. Her

teeth had felt like they were growing fuzz on them and she had stood in the shower with her mouth open.

"I'll take some coffee." He reached into the cabinet and took down a mug that read, *I Like Big Busts and I Cannot Lie* with a small police car underneath.

"You seem to know your way around my kitchen already. Care to explain?"

"Not really. You seem to have had a good time last night on that date. Care to explain?"

"Nope. But I will tell you about the mystery villain who was casing my house from the backyard last night."

"What, why didn't the birds…" Bernie didn't finish the sentence, catching himself.

"I'm catching on that more than one side is keeping tabs on me. I suppose I should be flattered?" She took the coffee from him and refilled her mug, blowing on the top for just a second before slurping it in anyway. "You're here early. I don't have time for bubble lessons this morning. I have to head to the day job. The Elemental side job will have to wait."

"That's a good one, Peabrain. Your side job can't wait." Bernie slapped his knee, letting out a snort, followed quickly by an eye roll. "Yeah, you better keep that day job. Pour me some of that in a go cup, will ya? Come on, your very life depends on it." He drained the mug of coffee, smacking his lips together.

"That's something I totally get but when this is all done, I'd still like to be employed and preferably at the job I really love. Not asking you to understand, still gonna' do it." Maggie reluctantly put down her coffee and grabbed her nearby purse, heading for the front door. "And you can pour your own coffee. Let's not pretend you haven't been all through this house when I wasn't looking."

"Then I'm coming with." Bernie put down the coffee and started walking toward the door, stopped by Maggie's outstretched arm, pushing him back.

"Not going to happen. I'm not walking into work with my elderly bodyguard."

"I'm still in my gnome prime. Don't be jealous."

"Yeah, that's my issue."

"I don't have to walk in like this. I can do fun size Bernie. Maybe a mouse. Plenty of those in Austin."

Maggie was already at the front door, holding it open. "Well, come on if you're coming. The El Camino is leaving in two minutes whether you're in it or not."

"Oh, hey great, didn't know it would be that easy. Hey, you don't look so hot. What did you do on your date last night? You know that saps your strength." Bernie was still following her down the front walk, lowering his chin and dropping his voice.

Maggie threw up her arms but didn't turn around. "There are way too many people involved in my life. Stick to helping me save the world, Bernie."

"Yeah, that seems easier." Bernie opened the door and slid in, already blowing bubbles, shrinking down to a grey field mouse, settling into the cup holder.

Maggie got in and shut the door behind her, pulling the seat belt across her chest. "Can you even talk when you're not gnome form? How does this work?"

The mouse looked up at her and twitched its whiskers but not much more. Maggie's eyebrows went up and she smiled.

"Really? Okay, lovin' this. Day seems a little better already." She started the car just as her phone buzzed and she looked down and saw it was a text from Jake.

'Thank you again for a great time last night. Still thinking about that kiss. Call you later.'

The feel of his mouth against hers came back to her and she smiled even more, pulling away from the curb. The mouse stood up on its hind legs, its paws resting over the edge of the cup holder.

"What?" asked Maggie. "My happiness throwing you off? Settle back, Bernie, we'll be at work soon."

CHAPTER EIGHTEEN

Maggie pulled into the parking lot at the precinct and scooped the mouse up, sliding him into her coat pocket without saying a word. He didn't have much choice. She wasn't going in there holding the mouse like it was a new fetish or a pet. She waved at the desk Sergeant and came down the hall, stopping long enough to fill up on more coffee.

"Mmmm, that's some good stuff." She breathed in deeply.

"Parker, you're the only cop I know who likes it better old and burnt." A senior homicide detective walked by her, shaking his head.

Maggie took a big slurp while trying to hold her mouth open to cool it off.

"Slow down there, chief," he said, moving past her.

She carried the coffee, blowing on the top and felt the mouse moving around in her pocket. It was too late to say anything or lay down some ground rules before they came inside. She was going to have to hope for the best.

"Hey Taylor, anything cooking?"

Her partner looked her up and down and arched an eyebrow. He sat forward in his seat, resting his elbows on his desk. "Little rough around the edges. You and the sister hang out at Mean Eyed Cat a little too long last night?"

"Something like that."

"Don't get too comfortable, we have a case. Robbery at an auto dealer."

"Someone steal a car?"

"More mundane than that. Broke in and stole the entire safe with the day's receipts. Did you know some people still pay for things in cash?"

"I had heard rumors like that." Maggie settled into her chair anyway, resting her hand against her pocket to keep the mouse from wriggling any further.

"There are cupcakes in the break room. O'Malley's wife brought them by for his birthday. I'm getting some now and we can take them with us. If I don't hustle, there won't be any by the time we get back."

"You move pretty well when you want to."

"Right motivation, partner, that's all it takes. I'll get you a couple too."

"We both know those are yours as well."

"Maybe, let's see how the day plays out."

The mouse inside her pocket struggled harder and Maggie pressed down, smiling at Taylor as he walked toward the break room set against the back wall surrounded by clear glass. There were already several detectives huddled around the table eating cupcakes in a few bites, stuffing their cheeks. "Man, they are not going to leave any!" Taylor picked up the pace.

"Hey, I can't breathe!" Bernie's voice erupted from her pocket.

Taylor turned, startled, looking around the fairly empty room. "You hear that?"

Maggie stared at Taylor, her eyes wide, saying nothing. She couldn't lie but it didn't mean she had to speak. She held her breath, not pressing down quite so firmly and waited. Two more detectives passed Taylor headed for the break room and he gave up, following close behind them.

"Thank you stars above for that man's appetite for sugar." Maggie gently scooped the mouse out of her pocket, opening her desk drawer just wide enough to set the mouse inside. "I thought you couldn't speak," she whispered. "Hey, how's it going?" She smiled at the patrol officer walking by, pulling a file over the drawer to provide cover and nodding as he looked over, puzzled.

Once he was gone, she pulled back the file and looked down at the mouse.

"I didn't say I couldn't, I just didn't say anything." Bernie's voice came out clear as a bell from the small mouse, even if it was at a lower volume.

Maggie's heart was pounding in her chest. "What next? Dude, this is freaking me out. It sounds just like you. Like Body Snatchers but weeble sized. You can't start talking like that. I have no way to explain it. No one is going to think I'm suddenly that good at ventriloquism. I can barely handle karaoke."

"You were smothering me. Be glad I'm not a real mouse. You must have been a prize in elementary school. Can't imagine a lot of class pets survived their weekend home with you."

Maggie frowned, brushing her hair out of her eyes. "You don't know that. You can't come on the call with me, especially if you might start talking. Taylor is older and has the worst diet. This might just do him in and I kind of like the guy. Don't hold up your little paw to protest. This is a hard no."

"Fine!" The small mouse crossed his arms over his hairy chest.

"Wait, you gave in too easy." Maggie looked up to see if Taylor was coming back yet, but she could see he was trying to eat a cupcake before grabbing a few more.

"No, I can see when it's pointless. Go take care of your business and I'll go looking for the compass. One of us has to look out for the world, keep the big picture in mind."

"I'll get you outside but that's the best I can do."

"No need." The mouse surprised Maggie and leapt out of the drawer. "I can take care of myself," he whispered, jumping onto the arm of the chair and scurrying down to the floor. He took off like a shot, dodging between feet and running over a shoe, making a sprint for the door just as another officer was coming inside. The mouse was out of the narrow opening just before the door slammed shut.

Maggie winced watching the last part, not wanting to see a flattened out Bernie.

"I brought you one." Taylor was in front of her, chocolate crumbs dribbled down the front of his shirt. He set a cupcake down in front of her. "That should help you get down the rest of that motor oil they call coffee around these parts."

Maggie stood up, feeling a little relieved. "I actually like the stuff."

"I know and the only explanation I have is too many years of you drinking blazing hot coffee. Your taste buds are dead, and your patience is not the best."

Maggie picked up the cupcake and made a move to leave.

"You going to eat that?" Taylor shrugged and tilted his head.

But Maggie gave a healthy lick to the top and smiled. "Yep, I am."

"Oh, come on, that wasn't necessary." Taylor grabbed his coat, sliding in his arms and grabbing the other two cupcakes as he hurried to catch up with Maggie. "Hey Fozzie, I'll take that point spread for Sunday. Put me down for fifty." Taylor waved at a detective, busy typing away on an iPad. The detective raised his head, nodding.

"I gotcha down, Taylor. Good luck to you."

"Isn't that illegal?" Maggie opened the door, feeling the rush of cold air. It felt good after the stuffy air inside.

"Nah, friendly wager between friends. That's still legal. Come on, Sanford's not my bookie. That would be illegal."

"Get in the car, and don't get any icing on my upholstery."

They pulled out of the parking lot in the El Camino and onto the street. Overhead a lone grackle followed closely, squawking loudly as it rode the currents of air. Other birds joined in formation, swooping and turning, trading messages and splintering into smaller groups, headed in different directions. The Huldus were watching over

Maggie Parker, doing their best to distract the Earth from noticing she was still alive.

CHAPTER NINETEEN

Maggie stood by the shiny new Santa Fe SUV, listening to the manager of the dealership tell the same story in a loop, while pointing to the broken glass in the front and the scrapes along the ground. She made a mental note that the hole in the front window wasn't big enough to drag the kind of safe they were talking about through the opening. From the look on Taylor's face, she knew he was thinking the same thing. Something wasn't adding up very well. *My new normal.*

"Sir, thank you, I appreciate your cooperation. I'd like to move onto a few other points of interest. Can we see the security tape?"

The manager shook his head hard, his well-coiffed hair not moving at all. He looked beside himself with worry. "That's what I'm trying to tell you. Our cameras," he said, flapping his arms before pointing at each of the well-positioned cameras, "are state of the art. State of the art! I made sure of that myself! But not one of them caught anything you can use. It's all grainy and the best you can see are blobs moving around something heavy. Had to be my safe."

"Stands to reason," said Taylor, giving Maggie a look. "Can we see this footage for ourselves?"

"Yes, yes, of course. If you think it will help." The man's face was shiny with sweat.

They got to the door of the office and Taylor hesitated. "Please enter first, sir." His hand was grazing his hip, close to his weapon.

Things were seeming eerily familiar to Maggie, too.

They followed the manager into the office and waited for him to pull up the footage. It didn't take long before they were staring at grainy film with blurry objects quickly moving something large.

"Five blobs it looks like." Taylor leaned in closer. "Can you stop it right there and enlarge that part?"

Maggie wrinkled her forehead and leaned in closer. "What did you see?"

"Sir, can you enlarge that right there, just a little more." Taylor tapped on the screen.

The manager gave a small grunt and leaned in sideways, tapping furiously as a small portion of the picture grew bigger. There in the center, barely visible if she hadn't seen something similar now twice before, was a cluster of stars in a random order. Maggie felt a chill down her spine and a tingle across the back of her neck.

Maggie's phone buzzed and she looked down to see her mother's name and the numbers 911 in a text. She felt her chest tighten. Even her mother never sent that kind of text without a good reason. "I'll be right back."

"What is it?" Taylor looked concerned, his hand now resting firmly on his gun.

"Not sure yet."

Maggie stepped outside of the office while Taylor put some distance between himself and the manager. He wasn't getting clocked twice in one week.

"Mom? Are you alright? Tell me what's happened. Slow down, I can't understand you." Maggie heard a buzzing in her ears, and she wasn't sure if it was the peabrain activating or if it was from what she was hearing. "Say it slowly, Mom."

Her mother pushed the air out of her lungs and did her best to breathe some back in. "These men showed up at our drumming. Came in from the alley and just came running right at me!" Her voice was strained. Maggie could tell she hadn't had a drink all day and felt for her. No morning glass of bourbon to get the day going. She was trying to stay clear to tell her what happened.

"The skinny one tried to pull out a gun, but Lucy beaned him with a drum. Got him good! She broke the drum on his head. That was an antique from up near Montana, I think!"

Maggie had to make herself stay in detective mode. She put her free hand on her hip, arching her back. *If you want to help her, do what you know how to do. Treat this like a case, first and hold her hand later.* Maggie clenched her teeth for a moment, holding herself back from trying to comfort her mother. It could only slow her mother down, distract her. *Not yet.* Still, it was taking everything she had not to soften her voice. Her mother was already having a hard enough time getting to the point.

"What is this neighborhood coming to? Break ins, yard invasions…" Toni Parker gulped in air, hiccupping from the effort.

"Is everyone alright, Mom?"

"No, no, didn't I say that already? Where was I? Dammit!"

"Who is hurt?" Maggie held her breath. *Please don't let it be Diana.*

"I don't know if anyone is hurt." Her mother's voice grew louder.

"You're not making sense, Mom." Maggie kept her voice low and calm. The seconds were ticking away. She waved her arm in the air at Taylor, signaling it was time to go. This crime would have to wait.

Toni spilled out the worst of it. "They took Kathleen, that nice old lady. She fought them off pretty well, but she got in the way. When they couldn't reach me, they grabbed her like some kind of second prize. I tried to stop them, but the others wouldn't let me. Penny scratched one of them and got a black eye for her troubles…" Her voice trailed off. "What do I do?"

"Wait inside for me and lock all the doors. I'm on my way. Where is Diana?" Maggie took off at a run for the door, shoving it open and sprinting for the car. They were coming for her family now. She wasn't enough anymore.

"She's on her way. I texted her too. Did I do enough?"

"Yes, you're still alive, Mom and we'll find Kathleen. I'm on my way."

Taylor saw the look on his partner's face and didn't ask anything else till they were on the road, sirens blaring. Maggie gunned the motor the entire way, leaning toward the steering wheel and weaving in and out of traffic. She made it across town in record time, taking the shoulder when necessary. The trees rustled as she passed, sending a message along the route. Someone had tried to harm a beloved of the Elemental.

A hard rain started up suddenly, blanketing the road and making it harder to see.

Maggie parked the El Camino in the first open spot along Pressler Street, the rear end still sticking out slightly. She killed the engine and got out and ran, grateful for all the miles she had already logged running around the neighborhood for exercise. Taylor moved surprisingly fast, keeping up at a good clip right behind her.

They got to the front of the yard and Maggie ran past the old live oak, stepping on the knotty roots above ground. A current of electricity ran through her, hitting her in the gut and practically knocking the wind out of her. She doubled over, stumbling over the roots and clenching her fists as she sucked in air. The trees were in shock, sending out a constant distress signal.

"Maggie, wait!" Taylor's gruff voice was a command. "Use your head. Doesn't help if we get sidelined." She looked back and saw Taylor ready, his gun drawn. Maggie took a deep breath, still gasping to fill her lungs and pulled out her gun. He nodded to her, his face grim and she turned and more slowly took the stairs, listening for anything out of place.

She went as quickly as she could through the front rooms.

"Clear."

There was a loud rustling from the kitchen and the sound of someone running. Maggie glanced back and saw Taylor's determined look, his gun raised as he hugged the wall. Maggie looked back in time to see her mother barreling toward her daughter's raised gun.

"Maggie! You're here!" Toni paid no attention to the gun, giving Maggie only moments to recover and pull the gun back, bracing for her mother's arm swinging around her neck, pulling her in close. She could smell the sour wine on her mother's breath.

"Mom, are you okay? Have you heard anything?"

Toni backed up, pressing her hands to her cheeks. "Taylor! You're here too."

"Mom, any calls?"

"No, no, nothing. I don't know what to do. Kathleen was trying to protect me!"

The radio on Taylor's hip buzzed and he nodded to Maggie as he headed for the front door. They had been partners long enough that a nod or a look would often do.

Diana came barreling through the kitchen door and into the hallway where they were all gathered. "The garage is secure, for once. The lock on the back gate is busted. They must have really kicked their way in."

"And it was so unnecessary! I always keep it unlocked."

Diana gave Maggie a look from behind their mother. "I can take Mom to my house."

"No, what if Kathleen comes back here?"

"Mom, what if someone else comes back here. Go with

Diana and let us do our job." Maggie hugged her mother again as Diana wrapped her arms around both of them. Maggie's gun was still in her right hand, hanging by her side. "I'll call as soon as I know something."

Taylor stepped back inside and lifted his chin, a dark look across his face. "Parker, we should get going and see if there's any news. Mrs. Parker, we'll turn up something."

Maggie let go, holstering her gun and grabbing Diana's arm, giving it a squeeze.

"I'll take good care of her. No one will get past me," said Diana. The same determined look Maggie had known all her life. The same one she had on her face. "I still have Dad's old gun collection, oiled and ready to go. Call out before you come in the house when you get back."

CHAPTER TWENTY

"Alright, tell me what you heard." Maggie was sliding into the driver's seat of the El Camino and closing the door in one swift move. The rain was still coming down and the sky was completely grey.

Taylor sat down hard with an oof, his hand holding on to the roof of the car. He pulled his leg in, reaching out for the door. "Hotshot call, priority zero. Something odd over in Garfield. There's a blaze going at the old abandoned rural hospital with reports of an older woman standing patiently out front. She matches your mother's friend's description. Hang on, that's not the strange part."

Maggie pulled away from the curb, already headed for Route 130. "This ought to be good," she said, through clenched teeth.

"The rain is coming down even harder over in Garfield and it's doing nothing to the fire. If anything, the blaze is burning brighter. Engine Company 1103 is out there throwing foam on it but so far, the chatter is nothing is working."

Maggie hit the lights and sirens, gripping the wheel. "Taylor, there are a few things I need to tell you."

Taylor shifted in his seat, the seat belt straining around his middle. "I don't know that now is the best time for true confessions."

"It has to be now and you're going to have to trust me."

Taylor's face turned red and he pressed his lips together for a moment. "When have I ever given you reason to believe I don't trust you." His head was bobbing from side to side like it did when he was really good and angry. "I know how to handle the weird and wonderful."

"This is gonna go a few feet beyond that. Remember how we got our clocks cleaned at that car museum?"

Taylor rubbed the back of his head. "Hard to forget. That future inmate was into some heavy tech."

"That wasn't technology, that was magic."

The red returned to Taylor's face. "If this is all some kind of elaborate practical joke, I'm asking for a new partner today."

Maggie held the wheel with her left hand and held out her right, doing her best to clear her mind and set an intention, all at the same time. Nothing happened. "Dammit!"

"What in Sam Houston are you doing?"

"Hang on!" Maggie swerved around a Volvo trying to get out of their way. "I don't know what we're walking into at the fire and it's not right to leave you in the dark." *Think of nothing and something.* She thought of Bernie's fireflies and opened her hand as small bubbles appeared with small glowing lights inside of them. The smell of magnolias filled the car.

Taylor pressed himself back against his car door even as he was leaning closer to get a better look. His eyes were wide, and his eyebrows knitted together. "You have got to be kidding me," he said in a hoarse whisper.

"Not at all!" A mouse popped up from the back seat, jumping onto the arm rest between the seats and standing on its hind legs, talking. Bernie had hidden away in the car, keeping watch over Maggie, just as he was instructed. "Magic is real," said Bernie, still residing in the form of a mouse, his whiskers twitching.

"Sumofabitch!" Taylor roared, spit flying from his mouth. He reached out with his large mitt of a hand and tried to swat Bernie toward the back window like he was up at bat and Bernie was a fur-covered ball. But Bernie was too fast for him, easily jumping out of the way.

Maggie swerved the car, jerking against the seat belt and trying to watch the road through the pouring rain and look at Taylor and Bernie.

"Did you see that too? Has your mother been smoking that crap so long it just hangs in her house waiting for someone to come through?" The veins were standing out on Taylor's neck and his hand was on his gun.

"I'm going to let that last comment go because it's possible it's true," said Maggie. "And because you look like you're stroking out. Take your hand off your gun. Listen to me, Taylor. Breathe in through your nose, come on, out through your mouth." Maggie glanced over at him and back at the road, zipping by as she tore down the road at eighty miles an hour. There was no time to pull over and let him adjust.

"Bernie, for the love of... Change into something else!

This is not how you let people know that magic exists." She realized she was shouting, trying to be heard over the rain and Taylor's string of swearing. It was some of the best he had ever done in all his life.

Large, translucent bubbles filled the car along with the scent of strawberries as the gnome appeared, full size sitting in the back seat of the car. "I don't believe we've met. My name is Bernie."

"Rule number two!" Maggie took the exit toward the center of Garfield and could already see the smoke rising above the horizon, despite the rain. *That has to be magical.*

"You were already breaking that one. I'm helping you out with some real proof. A nice party trick wasn't going to get the job done just before he literally has to jump into the fire. There's no time. A mouse turning into a gnome is perfect."

"Can someone fill me in on what the hell is happening? I'm going crazy, that's the only explanation."

Bernie shook his hand between the seats. "This is what happens with you Peabrains. You ignore the obvious for a dozen other excuses. Electricity gets invented, can't see that. No problem. Talk on a phone to someone on the other side of the world with no wires. Sure. One small mouse turns into a small man..." Bernie held up his hand. "Saying it before anyone else does. I know I'm small. I do basic bubble metamorphosis and the word crazy gets bandied about."

Maggie made her voice level. "You're not crazy. It turns out the world is even more complicated and weird than you knew."

"If you want to call it a world because technically..."

"Not now, Bernie! One fun fact to absorb at a time. Listen, Taylor, we're headed to a fire that may not really be a fire. At least not in the conventional sense. It may be driven by magic, which means we're in over our heads. There are some pretty wicked people after, well, me and that's why they stormed my mother's backyard."

They came screeching up to the edges of the fire behind all the fire engines and rescue squads. "Stay close on this one and be careful."

"I'm shooting whatever twitches funny."

"Great plan," said Bernie. "Leave the front door open for me, will ya? I can travel faster in another form and without anyone asking too many questions. Firemen love dogs." He was already blowing bubbles and ducking down below the windows as he changed into a black Labrador.

Taylor hesitated, his eyes still wide but he left the door ajar and stumbled forward, his hand pressed briefly against his chest. Maggie stopped and put her hand on his arm. "You okay?"

"I'll get there. And I grew up in the seventies. You'd think this would be easier."

Bernie squirmed out of the back seat, taking off at a run into the rain to circle the building and search for magical residue.

Maggie found a Lieutenant standing near the blaze, a puzzled look on his face, staring at the flames.

"I'm Detective Parker. It was my mother's house where they first showed up. Where is the old woman?"

"She's being tended to over by the rescue squad. The damndest thing."

Maggie hesitated running over to check on Kathleen.

She needed more information. "What do you know about who might have done this?"

The fireman scratched his elbow, still looking at the fire. "Not much. I've been a fire eater for over twenty years and I've never seen anything like this. It's like a blue flame fire but we can see the flames. So far, nothing we've done has quenched it and oxygen doesn't seem to be feeding it. Strangest thing. It's not getting worse and it's not going away."

"Anyone inside the building?"

"Not that we can find but I'm not letting my people search too far inside without knowing what the hell's going on." He looked at Maggie. "Your friend shouldn't be alive. Blaze with this intensity should have taken her out. None of this is making any sense. But if her story is accurate, the kidnappers didn't set the fire and yet, it still looks like arson."

Maggie saw Bernie, still in dog form, run past the trucks, circling the building. He was right, no one was paying him any attention. He seemed to be searching for something.

"Thank you," she said to the fireman, taking off at a run after Bernie. "Bernie, here boy, Bernie!"

The dog stopped and barked at her. "Not funny," said Bernie. "I'm not your boy."

Maggie ignored him, still hoping the kidnappers might be in the area, but already suspecting the answer. "Did you find anything?"

"It's Simon Wesley's people, alright. That sickly lavender smell is everywhere. Rain won't wash away evidence of magic. Can't you smell it?" Bernie raised his furry nose in the rain, smelling the air. "But they're long gone. They didn't set this fire, though. This is someone far more powerful than that motley bunch. Not a Peabrain at all."

"Any idea what kind of magical could create a fire that can't be put out?"

"No, and that's disturbing. Definitely not an elf or a fae, or even a wizard. Not even with a spell. Doesn't even have the residue of dark magic. That's what I expected to find. I could have sworn I'd seen everything on this ship. I'll have to go back to the library and consult the archives. Are you ready to get out of here? There's nothing more we can learn. I'll meet you back at the car." He took off at a run in the direction of the El Camino.

Maggie turned around, looking for the truck that held Kathleen and saw the light on and doors open in the one furthest from the fire. "Please let her be okay."

CHAPTER TWENTY-ONE

Maggie finally got to the rescue squad and found Kathleen sitting just inside one of the rescue trucks. She was soaked through from the rain and shivering in the cold despite the heat from the fire. It didn't matter. Relief washed over Maggie, quickly replaced by an uneasy feeling over how easily she was rescued, unharmed. "Are you alright?" That was when Maggie saw the bandages. *Not unharmed. I will find who did this. I will find who meant to do this to my mother.* Her fingers curled into a fist by her side.

Kathleen lifted her arm, waving gently. It was wrapped in white gauze. The emergency technician was carefully wrapping her other wrist. "I'm fine, I'm fine." The words spilled out of her in an excited, rapid tumble. "Strangest thing. Group of men, four of them, had me tied up pretty good with rope. Young, maybe thirties and they didn't look bold enough to pull off a kidnapping. They were marching around arguing, calling someone on the phone who was yelling at them even more." She shook her head wearily. "Out of the blue, my ropes started to spark." She held up the partially bandaged wrist, the gauze trailing down. "That's how I got free." There were angry red blisters in a neat line across her wrist. She followed Maggie's gaze and the scowl on her face. "They already gave me something for the pain. It could have been worse."

"Tell her how the fire grew to that." The technician glanced up, his forehead wrinkled and one eyebrow arched.

Kathleen tilted her head to the side, the flow of words starting up again. "No idea, really. One moment it wasn't there and the next, lines of flames were zipping along the floor and flashing up the walls. Like the fire had a mind of its own. Beautiful really." She raised her hands, wiggling her fingers and winced, gently lowering them back down. "You should have felt the heat. The doorway was covered in fire like some kind of apocalyptic archway to hell. The men were shouting mumbo jumbo, waving their hands around like that would do something. Finally, they just ran off. Definition of cowards."

"But you made it out okay…" The technician said it soothingly, patting her shoulder. He sat back, putting tape on her wrist to hold the bandages in place. He looked up at Maggie, still pressing down the last of the tape. "They found her coming out of the old maternity wing with a wet blanket over her head. Apparently, the water was never fully shut off to the place. Probably saved her life. There, all done. I've got to check on a firefighter, but I'll be back." He took off at a jog toward one of the fire engines. The fire was still blazing in the background.

Taylor came up to the truck, his coat pulled over his head in the rain. "No sign of anyone. Not even tire tracks and in this mud that's not possible. The general consensus is the kidnappers didn't set the fire, so there should be plenty of tire tracks out here. Not sure how they got out of here unless they lifted off in a helicopter. The bad guys are getting way too smart." He pursed his lips looking around the scene. Maggie knew he was looking for any kind of plausible explanation other than magic so he could just forget the car ride over there.

"Let's get you home, Kathleen." Maggie put her hand under Kathleen's elbow to help her stand.

"I want to check on your mother, first. Let's go by there."

"She's okay, you don't need to do that."

"I insist. After all they were originally after Toni. I'm not sure they knew what to do with me. That seemed to be the whole argument before the place went up in flames. I'm not going to rest easy until I lay eyes on her. You'll find I can be quite stubborn, Miss Maggie. Come on, let's go before that nice fellow gets back. He seems to think I'm an old lady."

Maggie gave a tight smile. "I'm so sorry this happened to you."

Kathleen leaned on her as they made their way through the rain, weaving among the firemen and trucks to the car. Bernie was already in the backseat.

Taylor caught up with them when they were almost to the car. "I found nothing. They were thorough even if they did run away quickly. The fire took care of a lot of it for them." He stopped, his face frozen in mid-sentence when he saw Bernie sitting in the back seat, once again in gnome form. He hesitated, wiping the rain off his face and turned his back to the car.

Maggie helped Kathleen into the backseat, settling in next to Bernie. She went to the trunk and found a blanket, depositing it in the back. "Wrap up in this, it's way too cold out here."

Kathleen sniffed the air, wrinkling her nose. "Why does it smell like wet dog? You don't have a dog, do you?"

Maggie opened her mouth to say something but gave up. Bernie shrugged and helped pull the blanket around Kathleen, introducing himself. "Bernie, nice to meet you. You new in town?"

Taylor was still leaning against the car. He seemed to be arguing with himself, weighing out something.

"Taylor, its real and it's okay." Maggie had to talk over the rain. "Just because we didn't know about it doesn't mean there's something wrong. Think of it like a new and amazing invention. Like discovering how to make a plane fly."

"This is a bit more complicated." He looked at the fire. "And deadly. What's going on here, Parker? You in trouble?"

"The first answer is going to take a while. Magic is real and the world is not what we thought, but we'll figure it out. The second answer is yes, I'm in trouble and I'll figure that one out too."

"We'll figure it out, together. Don't go cutting me out of the greatest case I'll see in my career." He gave her a crooked smile she knew was meant to encourage her.

"Let's get out of the rain. I'm freezing and there's nothing here for us to learn. Once we drop off Kathleen, I'll tell you about strange bubbles and a missing compass and a passenger ship that got off course."

"I couldn't have called the odds on this." Taylor shook his head, wearily, rain dripping off the end of his nose.

"You're right, Taylor. We'll figure this out together, over a beer, on me."

Maggie opened his door, doing her best to give him a reassuring smile, blinking in the rain.

"I don't know about that Bernie," he whispered, before sliding into the car and glancing into the backseat. Bernie and Kathleen were busy chattering away about bluebonnets in the spring. Bernie's excitement was spilling over, and he hiccupped a few small fireflies, covering his mouth.

Taylor startled, shaking his head.

"I'm not so sure about any of it," said Maggie just before she shut his door, jogging over to the driver's side. She was soaked to the skin, shivering, but her mind was racing.

Magic was a part of her life from the moment she was born, whether she had known or not. This was always her normal. A new definition of normal. "Too bad it wants me dead." A shiver ran through her hard enough to shake her as she got in the car, settling in for the drive to her mother's house.

She looked down at her watch and saw that it wasn't even noon yet. "Man, these days are getting longer and longer."

"You said it, partner." Taylor rested his head back and stared straight ahead.

She started the car and began to pull out, looking in the rear-view mirror at the fire. She noticed that the further they got away from the fire, the more the flames seemed to be dying down, giving into the rain. *Something is controlling the fire. Are they watching me leave?*

CHAPTER TWENTY-TWO

T oni was waiting at her house. She wouldn't let go of Kathleen once she saw the bandages and the wet clothes. She insisted on outfitting Kathleen with warm, fuzzy clothes and making impromptu s'mores over the gas burner. Just like when Maggie and Diana were little. Toni was at her best in a crisis or a sudden celebration. Oscar followed Kathleen around the house, nuzzling against her and wagging his tail.

"I have to get Taylor back to the station and into dry clothes." A pool of water was forming around his feet. "I'll check back with all of you later."

Bernie had hung back in the car, waiting for Kathleen to get out of sight before he filled the car with bubbles drying it out. The smell of strawberries was everywhere, replacing the smell of wet Labrador. By the time Taylor and Maggie got back to the car the rain was letting up and the sun was showing through some of the clouds.

"We should circle back to the dealership and finish

getting the information on that robbery," said Maggie. "It felt like that was days ago instead of just a few hours."

"My mind is kind of fried. I tagged Moss a while ago while we were still at the fire and told him this would make us even on the Giants game. He still owed me a large for that one, and he was more than happy to work it off by just doing his job. Can you drop me at home? I'm gonna grab lunch with Claire and talk about how I should pick up after myself more, eat a little tuna fish salad. I'll meet you back at the station in an hour. I can get Claire to drop me off. I'll tell her it was a helluva morning. She never asks too many questions."

"Sounds like a plan."

Bernie chimed in from the backseat. "Ditto."

"Oh geez." Taylor slapped his hand to his face. "Maybe you can be done with your ride along by the time I get back to the station." He went to put on his seat belt but stopped and twisted in his seat to look at Bernie. "And no sneaking on board as a mouse or a cricket or something else that is suddenly going to start speaking the king's English to me." He was stabbing the air with a thick finger, emphasizing the words. "I think I've been pretty accommodating up to now but I'm gonna need a day to absorb all of this."

"Seems fair." Bernie slid back in his seat, shrugging at Maggie, mouthing, 'sensitive'. Maggie glared at Bernie in the rear-view mirror and started up the El Camino. The light shone brightly into the car as she pulled away and the trees gently swayed in her direction as the car passed down Pressler. A sense of momentary calm came over her and the memory of talking to the trees while holding her father's hand flashed through her mind again. *This has always been who I am, just forgotten.*

———

"I'm hungry." Bernie had moved up to the front seat of the El Camino and was straining against the seat belt looking out the front window like he was trying to get somewhere faster.

"We have to look for the compass. Too many weird things are happening. You said the book needs to be checked again to figure out who's the fire starter. Let's do that first."

"I'm not going to last too much longer without food. Take me somewhere or I bubble on out of here to the cafeteria near the engine room. Today's meatloaf day and I'm not thrilled about missing it in the first place."

"I'll make you a deal. One hour searching for the compass and then I'll take you to Hopdoddy's. I'll even buy. The breakfast burger can make me forget a lot of troubles. It'll be worth the wait, I promise, and we might even get closer to saving the world before lunch, or maybe just my hide."

"I like that ambition, Peabrain, but I don't know. If it's not Huldu meatloaf, then it's gotta be Subway. Perfect place to eat. You can get practically anything between two slices of bread, done your way. You could even order one with rabbit food."

"That's always an option, but no." Maggie pulled into the lobby of the library. "One hour, now show me how to get through that wall again."

"One hour and this place better have milkshakes."

"Puhleez. I'm not an amateur. You want a Nutella chocolate pretzel shake or a strawberry shortcake shake? I'm from these woods, mechanic, and I don't eat rabbit food."

"Okay, simmer down. I get it. Fine, you have a deal but bring your wallet. Gnomes are not nibblers."

Maggie went through the drive thru of a McDonald's on their way over there to get a Happy Meal. She parked near the dumpster and got out, spotting his shopping cart hidden behind it but Slim was nowhere to be seen.

"Too early in the day. Leave it for him in his cart. It'll be cold, he'll complain and eat it anyway. It's our schtick. What's the prize?"

Maggie opened the box and looked inside. "A Teen Titan, whatever that is."

"Oooh, is it Beast Boy? I don't have that one yet."

Maggie tilted her head to the side. "I'm not giving you his prize. He'll know."

"He's homeless, he doesn't need more stuff."

"You live underground, neither do you." Maggie tucked the Happy Meal under an old, stained towel in the cart.

"You wound me, Peabrain. Come on, let's head inside."

They made their way inside and through the library, up the

stairs and got to the far wall back in a corner where very few patrons ever went.

Bernie pulled Maggie through the wall with a pop and she let out a giggle of delight. "That doesn't get old."

"You've done it twice. Do you do that every time you walk through a doorway? Peabrains," he said, shaking his head. "Amazed by the invention of the toaster. How about we calm down and see how you feel after a few hundred times? Come on, your one hour is ticking down." Bernie made a beeline for the purple tome and licked his finger, flipping pages furiously, scanning them briefly and flipping more of them. "That can't be. There's nothing in here. Less than nothing! The old writings say it's impossible to control fire. Practitioners of dark magic have tried for centuries, of course. Who doesn't love a little arson to make your evil point? But it always goes south and kaboom! Krakatoa!"

"Well, clearly the book is wrong." Maggie leaned over his shoulder, reading the page.

Bernie tapped the page, incensed. "The book is *never* wrong. Maybe incomplete because of that other little fire in Egypt but not wrong. No one has seen anyone success-fully control fire like that since the Library of Alexandria was burned." He threw up his hands. "It's a mystery. But whoever it was has a beef with Simon and his followers."

"Only question we need to answer is if the beef is with all Peabrains or just his Scooby gang." Maggie turned around and looked at the stacks of other books. She went down one aisle, reading off the spines. *Herbal Healing Reme-dies. Bubbles for Beginners. Portals Made Easy. Understanding The Elementals.* She ran her hand over the raised gold

MARTHA CARR & MICHAEL ANDERLE

letters on the spine of the last book and pulled it off the shelf. "What's this?"

"What?" Bernie looked up from the tome, still turning pages. "My cousin, Billy wrote that just in case we were ever able to find you guys."

Maggie opened the book and read from the page. "Each Elemental is important but only one is necessary. Hey, can I check this out?"

"It's not that kind of library. The answer is no. You can read it here, but you have to leave it behind. I know you said you have a thing about lying but just in case that doesn't extend to stealing, let me save you the trouble. There are wards all over this room and if you try to take a book, you'll get a shock like you never felt. Goosed by magic. The book stays behind, and you go through the wall to the other side. Punishment for even trying is banishment from the room for a month and we don't have the bandwidth for you to be making those kinds of mistakes."

"Got it, no borrowing books." She looked down and kept reading. "It says here I'm connected to the compass." She looked up at Bernie, her finger still on the page. "Then I should be able to sense where it's located."

"That's the rumor but without a guide like the last Elemental, I have no idea how to help you tune into that. That was one of those secrets an Elemental's not supposed to tell just anybody."

"And it died with my father..." Maggie gently closed the book and put it back on the shelf.

"Sorry kid. I'm hoping nature will kick in at some point and you'll just, you know, kind of naturally figure out how to handle this gig." He held his hands out to the side.

"There's going to be some assembly required." He pointed at Maggie. "Maybe the trees can help. They won't talk to anybody but you, the mother ship and a few million insects and they see everything. One giant network that covers the entire ship. They have to know a few things."

"I know you're trying to help, it's okay Bernie. We'll figure this out." She let out a deep sigh, not realizing she was holding her breath. "In time," she whispered, looking at the rows of books. "We'll figure it out in time."

"Let's get out of here. We need some fresh air." Bernie took Maggie firmly by the hand and walked them both through the wall. "Time for some eats." He glanced at the solemn look on Maggie's face. "You know, some of my best noodling over a problem happens if I'm willing to take a break. My mind keeps working on it somewhere in the back." He circled the top of his head with his finger. "Boom, out pops an idea. A little food couldn't hurt either."

"Sounds a little self serving," said Maggie as they headed back down the stairs.

"Best ideas serve both sides."

"You and Taylor really should be friends."

"Takes Peabrains a while to warm up to me, but most generally do. I'm a likeable guy. Now tell me more about that Nutella shake."

CHAPTER TWENTY-THREE

They stood in the long line at Hopdoddy's on South Congress right by the line of pictures of local musicians who had made good. Bernie was busy studying the menu, or talking to people in line, or admiring the full stocked bar across the room from where they stood.

"This is my kind of playground!" He whistled through his teeth, his eyes wide in amazement. "I have really spent too much time in our cafeteria. Who knew? There's even a bar!"

"Huldus can drink, that's a new thought." Maggie smiled at Bernie, despite the dozens of thoughts racing through her mind. *He's right, I can use a distraction.*

"Yeah, but not really a good one. Woof! Imagine a few hundred wild-eyed magicals who can pack some muscle. Remember that snowmageddon a few years back? Holiday party and someone had snuck in some hooch. We got a little carried away at the controls. Louie even hit the snow lightning button. That one doesn't get used very often." Bernie shrugged. "It happens. Chicago dug out eventually and everyone has something to talk about. Hello, how ya doing?" Bernie nodded to the tall young man with a bushy blonde beard and short cropped hair, standing behind him.

The gnome looked him up and down, sizing him up. "Your family go way back?"

Maggie's phone chirped and she looked down to see a text from Jake. *Long day at work. Are you free Friday night? Let's get dinner. We can talk football all night.* Maggie smiled and leaned over to whisper to Bernie, "He's not a Kashgar. Most of the world is taller than you are."

Bernie pursed his lips sizing up the young man.

"Hey little dude." The burly young man put out his hand to Bernie and tipped his brown pork pie hat.

"Oooh, I can't look." Maggie turned her back and typed a message. *It's a date. I'll show you my brackets if you show me yours.* She smiled at her own joke. Her head popped up, suddenly processing what she was hearing in the background.

"I'm tall for my kind, I'll have you know, and I can lift kindling like you over my head," said Bernie, with a low growl.

Maggie slid her phone into her pocket and wheeled around in time to stop Bernie from power hugging the young man and lifting him high overhead. The man was smiling at Bernie and elbowing his friend next to him. "You in a cover band, some kind of dead head? That's cool," he said.

Bernie hiccupped, cupping his mouth with his hand. A few small fireflies fluttered from behind his fingers.

"Whoa, dude! That is awesome! You're a magician.

Alright, alright," he said, bobbing his head. "What else can you do?"

"Leave it alone, Bernie. Come on, we're next."

Bernie opened his mouth and blew a large bubble. Floating inside was a rainbow that changed color as the bubble turned.

"Isn't that breaking rule number two?" whispered Maggie.

"No, Peabrains always assume it's a trick of some sort."

A man with long, string hair wearing a t-shirt and cargo shorts elbowed past the young man. "You have anything better? That's just a rainbow. I can do a rainbow."

Bernie opened his mouth again, a scowl crossing his face, but thought better of it and turned around.

Maggie looked over at him in amazement, wrinkling her forehead. "Wow, that's... that's progress Bernie. You let something go."

"Every once in a while, I like to do that. Besides, there wasn't much I could do without breaking rule number one. Never harm a Peabrain. That one is unbreakable. There's only one exception to that first rule."

"This is like a cliffhanger. Just tell me, Bernie."

"If they try to harm an Elemental. Then all bets are off." Bernie sniffed the air. "Besides, he's not a Kashgar. I don't smell any cherries. Signature scent of Kashgar magic."

Maggie sniffed the air, wondering if she'd smell something but all she smelled were hamburgers cooking on a grill. Her stomach growled in response and she realized all she'd had was the coffee in the morning. *Not even enough coffee.*

"Next!" The young woman in a dark blue t-shirt that

MARTHA CARR & MICHAEL ANDERLE

read, *Open Wide*, smiled brightly at them as Maggie and Bernie stepped up to the cash register. "What do you want, Bernie? It's on me. I'll take the breakfast burger with a side of habaneros and an order of fries. You have Mexican coke, right? A large no ice." She pointed to Bernie and herself. "We're both on the same ticket."

"How nice, is your grandpa new to Austin?"

Maggie gave a crooked smile and refused to look at Bernie.

"I'm not her grandfather. More like a teacher. Habaneros, really? Living large, Elemental. We're riding back to your place with the windows down." Bernie scratched the top of his head.

"That's just a Texas pickle. Come on, order already. You can get what you want. I found some quarters in my couch cushions."

"Very funny. This is gonna take some plastic. Have you seen those prices? Do you know how much we could get at Subway for that?"

"You want me to order for you?"

"Don't rush me." Bernie scanned the menu, running his finger down the different burger choices. "El Diablo, no, no." He patted his belly, wincing. "Veggie burger? What's the point? I'll take the Goodnight burger but hold the jalapenos and extra caffeinated BBQ sauce. That is a dream come true. And one of those malted root beer shakes. Don't be chintzy with the malt ball toppings. I love this place!" Bernie turned around and slapped the man behind him on the back, jostling him. "You're next!"

Maggie and Bernie made their way to a high-top table near a window. Bernie hopped up into the chair, already tapping his fingers, looking back and forth between the people sitting outside and the counter at the other end of the large room. A waiter finally approached with a tray and Bernie slapped the table in delight.

Bernie took a look at the sausage, ham, beef, egg, bacon, cheese and potato burger in front of Maggie and let out a grunt. "You really can pack it away, Peabrain. You've got all the major meat groups covered there."

"No chicken," said Maggie, opening wide to take a big bite.

"I said major groups. Come here bad boy."

Neither one of them said much till there was nothing left but a few stray burned fries. "My favorite ones," said Maggie, crunching them between her teeth.

Bernie wiped his mouth with the last of the napkins. "Tell me something, why did you want to become a cop. That's usually a good story."

Maggie's expression darkened and she dropped the last of the fries, brushing her hands. "It's a long story."

"So, give me the short version. We have a few minutes before we run back out there for the next adventure. Humor me. We should bond more if we're going to be on this quest together. What's your origin story?"

Maggie looked out the window into the distance. "I wanted to change the world, but not the way most people mean when they say that. I wanted to change one particular story and find a happy ending."

"The one with your father?"

A shock of pain shot across Maggie's face. "No, that story can't be changed. It had a very final ending. I'm talking about my best friend since I was five years old. I was one of the younger five-year olds in kindergarten and wasn't sure of the lay of the land. Everything was a little scary."

"For you? You're the original, how about we try this and find out later if we should or not. I pictured you sticking things in sockets and taking umbrellas up to the roof to fly."

"I was that kid and I have the scars to prove it, but people have always been a different kind of deal. But my classroom had this enormous coat closet and when being around people got to be too much, I would go stand in it for a few minutes. It was a refuge, particularly in the winter when it was cold out and the closet would be full of warm, wool coats."

"There's a point here, right? I know I live for thousands of years…"

Maggie clenched her jaw and stopped talking.

Bernie saw his mistake and pursed his lips for a moment. "Sorry, there's the line. I generally have to stomp on top of it to even see it."

Maggie didn't say anything and went back to staring out the window.

"Go ahead, I was the big shot who said we should bond. I tell you what, I'll even listen as if my mind can be changed. Okay?" Bernie ducked his chin down, tilting his head to the side and attempting a toothy grin, whistling his words through his teeth. "I really am sorry this time, no kidding. I want to hear your story. When we last left you, you were five and in the closet."

Maggie smiled just a little and looked back at the

gnome. "You're horrible but you're growing on me like a pleasant-smelling mold."

"I deserved that." He put his elbows on the table and rested his chin in his laced fingers, saying nothing.

Maggie let out a sigh. "Fine, I was in the closet at five, have it your way." Maggie leaned on the table. "Halfway through the school year there was a new girl in the class. Her name was Stephanie and she had this long, blonde braid she would swish around."

"Like that Frozen chick."

"Yes, exactly like her. Everyone liked her instantly and she seemed to get along with everyone else. But one afternoon when everyone else was busy learning their alphabet, I went into the cloak room and there was Stephanie with a flat stick, eating the paste out of big plastic jar. Her anxiety was worse than mine, but she hid it better, till she didn't."

Bernie sat up straighter. "A story with a twist. She was a secret paste eater. Go on."

"She looked at me, horrified like I could make things a whole lot worse, but frankly, my dad was dead, and my mother was chemically enhanced. I had no desire to make anything worse for anyone. I told her I'd keep her secret and sat there with her quietly while she swallowed a few more mouthfuls."

"You tried some, didn't you?" Bernie sucked on the straw from his shake as hard as he could, getting a mouthful. "Ahhhh, that's good."

"Of course I did. That's what friends do. It wasn't bad. It didn't taste like anything. We became good friends after that. Turned out her life at home was not that different from mine. We went everywhere together and slept over at each other's house all the time. Our families took to calling us the twins." Maggie sat back in her seat, reluctant to go on.

"This is where the story takes a turn I'm not going to like." He squeezed his eyes shut for just a second. "Okay, hit me with it."

"It was when we were in fifth grade and it was spring. Time for the annual Easter egg hunt in a large field on the southeast side of Austin at the end of William Cannon Drive. Our last year we could participate, and we were so excited about it. The older kids had five eggs that had five-dollar bills in them." Maggie's bottom lip trembled, making Bernie feel a sudden surge of anger for whoever did this to her, surprising himself.

"Now there's a big subdivision but back then there was nothing," she said, looking back out the window, brushing her dark hair out of her eyes. "We set off together with our baskets but there were hundreds of kids and so many eggs and I saw her when I got to an old live oak. I got to the egg first and she was laughing, that braid flying across her back. Then I saw her again in the middle and we compared baskets for just a second. I think we were about even. But it wasn't long before I lost sight of her. I wasn't worried, we had a job to do. We both wanted to find those five eggs. We were saving up for tickets to Comicon." The words spilled out of Maggie. They had lived deep inside of her for so long that she had forgotten they were there, waiting for a voice.

"I was a comic book junkie. DC comics mostly, old school. Wonder Woman was my favorite. That lasso of truth and invisible plane. Stephanie got it. Every good memory I have of my childhood, there's Stephanie standing next to me, smiling. You know, she was even braver than I was once she had me by her side."

A silence fell over the table and for once, Bernie didn't speak. He sat there patiently, waiting as if there was all the time in the world and the earth was just the earth and there wasn't a compass out there or Kashgars hunting down Elementals.

A tear rolled down Maggie's cheek and she felt the old urge pull at her to put the memories away and just get on with things. But something happened to her inside of the tree, listening to the world talking, without interruption, saying everything it had seen, passing on every message it received. "It was the end of the day and that's when I realized something was wrong." Her voice dropped to a whisper, but she took a deep breath and started again, her voice gaining strength. She cleared her throat and wiped her face with a napkin stained with grease. "I realized something was wrong when she didn't come looking for me. Her mother asked me where she was and for the first time since that closet when I was five years old, I had no answers. I had no idea."

"Can I get y'all anything?" The smiling waiter was back.

"Really? Read the room, dude and run away." There was just the edge of venom in his voice and the smile slid off the waiter's face as he looked at Maggie. "Sorry," he muttered, backing away.

Maggie pressed her hands flat against the table. *Don't stop until you finally say the words this time. Do it!*

"We searched all night. They even let me stay out there, looking everywhere. No one could have stopped me anyway. But we never found anything except her basket, abandoned in the woods and still full of eggs. That was it. It was like she was beamed up somewhere. But she was gone and eventually they said she had to be dead." Maggie lifted her chin and looked at Bernie.

"She was murdered, and we held a service with no body. After that I stuck by my sister and we did everything together. It was easier. And I wanted to keep the people I love safe so…"

"Being a police officer was a natural choice." Bernie finished the sentence for her. "And crap has found you anyway." He shook his head, weary.

Maggie bit her bottom lip and took in a long, even breath. "There's something important I've learned along the way. Crap is going to find you no matter what you do. It's what I do when it arrives that matters, and I'll tell you something, I don't run. I don't even stand still. I go light the situation up and deal with it, and that's just what we're going to do for as long as I can until the Earth snatches me back."

Bernie wiped his nose with his shirt and took in a breath that sounded more like a snort, slapping the table hard. "Well that's not going to happen. Not on my watch, by Huldu! I'll be your paste eater."

Maggie's eyes filled and she felt an old weight lift off her shoulders.

Bernie took an old handkerchief out of his pocket that looked like it'd seen better days, handing it over. The words were spilling out of him and he was pounding his fist into his hand. "Let's get out of here, we have a compass to find and a ship to program, somehow." He was already scrambling out of his chair. "I'm really not sure about that last part but there has to be a way and we'll find it. We'll talk to the trees, or you will. Things won't talk to me. I'll get all my cousins on this, we'll find that compass! Why have we been doing this by ourselves, anyway?"

Maggie slid off her seat, brushing another tear off her cheek. She gave a small smile at Bernie's retreating back as he marched toward the door, still making declarations. "Out of our way, we have important business!"

She got to the car and stopped. "Hey Bernie, thank you."

"Any time, kid. You're the Elemental and I've been assigned to you. Oh hell, I may even like you. Come on, let's get going. We have to find a compass and get ahead of the Kashgars, those tall bastards." Bernie got in the car, back to talking a mile a minute. "You want to talk about evil on this ship. Now there's some pretty nasty business."

Maggie got in and started up the El Camino, pulling out of the parking lot, still feeling a little bit lighter but determined, more than ever to keep everyone she loved safe. Maybe even Bernie too. *Time to find a compass, save the world.*

CHAPTER TWENTY-FOUR

"This is everything." Maggie brushed her hair out of her face and put her hands on her hips. "If I'm from a long line of Elementals then something should be in here, right?"

"That's the theory." Bernie smoothed out the front of his red and blue striped woolen sweater.

"Where are you getting those sweaters from?" Maggie held up her hands. "No judgment, just curiosity. Gift exchange?"

"I'm a sweater connoisseur. Slim helps me find them."

"Ah, question answered. When is your birthday?"

"No need, I like to pick these things out for myself. Otherwise, what's the point? Now can we get back to why we're here? I'm pretty sure my fashion choices are low on the list."

"Still, when we're done here, I may have something in the attic."

"Whatever does it for you, kid. I can always give it to

MARTHA CARR & MICHAEL ANDERLE

Jack. Although he's more of a sports coat kind of gnome. The boxes?"

They stood in the center of Maggie's study surrounded by boxes covered in dust. Bernie pushed the closest one with the toe of his shoe.

"That's black mold, isn't it? I think that's black mold. Where were you keeping these things?"

Maggie pressed her lips together and brushed her hand against the box, making Bernie recoil. "Peabrain, that's not good! That stuff can get in your skin."

"Relax, Huldu, it's dirt. Good old fashioned, solid composted dirt. These were out in the garage, high and dry. I'm surprised you didn't trip over them during your break in." She arched an eyebrow, giving him a determined look.

"Hey, it was necessary, and I was focused on other things. I had no idea I should be looking for clues to the home game of *What's My Line*."

Maggie crouched down and opened the nearest box. The side was creased in a downward slope and the tape was covered in small bits of dirt. On the top was written, *Poppy* in black magic marker.

She put her hand inside and pulled out a few books. "These were my grandfather's. He's the one who taught Dad to love books. Dad was a bookaholic and it used to drive Mom crazy. Well, crazier. I saw him sneak books in the house in his pockets or if they were small enough, up his coat sleeves and then leave them in a pile like they were here all along."

"I want to let this caring moment brought to us by Random House go on and on, but I feel the pressure of time and I'm a gnome. Not normally an issue. Can we focus a little?"

"You snap back to your usual banter pretty easily."

"Thousands of years tends to make something a habit." Bernie went to open a box and Maggie shot out an arm, trying to slow him down. "Wait!"

Bernie looked up and rolled his eyes. "I promise I'll be careful." He held up three fingers in the Boy Scout salute. "This means something to you Peabrains, right? Okay, then." He carefully opened the box, wincing with a hiss when part of the box tore, but he didn't slow down. Inside were rows of old VHS tapes carefully lined up. "Hello 1980's, how are you? Ooooh, lookie here. TV shows, dozens of them and he's got some good ones here. Knight Rider, Miami Vice and bingo! Come to papa, Golden Girls." He let out a delighted hiccup and a few tiny bubbles filled with momentary fireflies.

"Who's getting distracted now? Stop manhandling the Golden Girls and keep looking for clues."

"Meh, I'll save this for a break." He set the tape aside, giving it a soft tap and a satisfied smile.

"A lot of good it'll do you. The player has been broken since Pops died in 1997." She pointed to the old relic on a shelf gathering dust. "It's more of a conversation piece at this point. Mom was thinking of making it into art. I should give it to her, keep her amused for a day or two, maybe even a week."

"I'm a mechanic, Parker, I can fix anything." The words whistled through his teeth.

"Keep hunting. If being an Elemental was that big of a

deal and Dad died leaving a void, then Pops had to have left an instruction booklet or a note."

"There's nothing here. I'll try the next box."

Hours passed with nothing to show for it. They had even moved on to searching through old family pieces of furniture to see if anything was hidden away. Still nothing. Finally, Maggie sat back, discouraged and covered in dirt, a smear down her cheek. She looked toward the window and the setting sun.

"I'm going to order food. It's getting to be about dinner time."

"That side of every animal between a bun isn't sticking with you?" Bernie was laying on his back, looking up at the bottom of a large, dark wooden desk, pushing on every surface he could find. "For the love of... nothing at all! How could someone leave nothing about being an Elemental?"

Maggie ignored him, not wanting to think about any of the long gone anymore, at least for a little while. It was as if they had let her down again by leaving her alone to figure things out. She stood up, brushing off her jeans and moving her jaw side to side and left the room without another word.

"Wait!" Bernie banged his head sitting up too fast. "Ooof, order me something too. What are we doing, Subway? Chinese? Mexican? How about Mexican?"

Maggie waved her hand in the air without turning

around and went to the kitchen to dig through the drawer of old menus.

Bernie stayed behind and pulled the VHS player off the shelf, blowing on the top and sending a puff of dust into the air. He blinked, his eyes watering and let out a sneeze filled with small bubbles. Each one contained a dandelion and as they popped, the seeds of the dandelions blew around the room in a swirl. "Well, that's a first."

The gnome gripped the edge of his sleeve and wiped his arm across the player, taking away most of the dirt and few remaining dandelion seeds. "Need a screwdriver, looks like a Phillips head. Should be called a Bernie head because I'm pretty sure I was using one of these long before this Phillips guy."

He looked up to see Maggie staring at him, puzzled.

"What? I work better if I keep the conversation going and you left the room. Do your thing, I'll have this fixed in no time."

"I'll be in the kitchen."

"I'll be in here expounding on the wonders of this ship. Might miss something."

"I'm sure there will be other opportunities," she called from down the hall. Maggie went out her kitchen door to feed the chickens, heading for the garage. The chickens came out of their house greeting her loudly and running down the wire fencing with her.

Inside the garage, she found the old yellow bucket and the bags of feed against the wall and took off the clip keeping one of the bags shut. She reached inside for the blue scoop and filled the bucket, feeling herself reset. Getting back to doing whatever the next right thing was always did that to her. She went outside to the coop and opened the gate, going inside and shutting it behind her. The chickens swirled around her feet, keeping up their chatter as she made her way to their trough and poured out the feed in a steady line.

Maggie stood back when she was done and looked at all the chickens standing next to each other, busy pecking at the feed and felt a sense of satisfaction. "You guys aren't worrying about what might come next or who isn't here anymore. You're eating and all is right with your world." She looked up at the Texas sky and the swirl of red and purple behind the clouds.

She made her way out of the coop and put back the bucket, locking up the garage and heading back to the house. But as she passed the old live oak in the backyard she paused and put out her hand, slowly and gingerly touching the bark. A hum immediately picked up and traveled through her body. "I can hear you."

Red elms along Reserve Road need assistance. Not enough water.

Trouble spotted on Sixth Street near Lamar Boulevard.

Winds picking up along Atlantic Avenue.

She shut her eyes and listened to the steady stream. "You're the newscasters for Mother Earth, reporting back to the ship about everything, not just the trees. But are you just observers?"

"Maggie! Maggie, come here!" Bernie interrupted her reverie and she pulled her hand back abruptly, cutting the connection. The buzz immediately died down and went quiet.

She let out a brief sigh and headed to the house, taking

the stairs two at a time. "What is it? Is the food here?" She grabbed her purse from the kitchen counter as she came down the hall and looked in the study, but Bernie was nowhere to be seen and the front door was closed.

"Bernie?" She found him in the living room staring up at the TV mounted on the wall, a remote in his hand. The VCR was balanced on a bookshelf, connected to the back of the TV and on the screen was Poppy, Maggie's grandfather, saying her name. "Where did you find this?" She stared, mesmerized by the sound of his voice. *I had forgotten what he sounded like.*

"I didn't exactly. Turns out your old Poppy was a little clever. I popped in the Golden Girls tape and this is what started. He must have known just how powerful this show was for others."

Maggie tilted her head to the side, her eyebrows raised. "That's what you're going with?"

"It's obvious really. Shhhhh, he's saying something to you. Hold on, I'll rewind it a little. Do you think this means no Golden Girls?"

"Get a Netflix account."

"Terrible reception underground. Okay, here we go, watch this part in particular."

"This is your codex, Maggie, for being an Elemental, at least a partial one. I'm sorry I didn't do more to record all of this for you, but your dad died pretty suddenly, and I..." His voice trailed off for a moment and he looked pained. "I don't have enough time left to do this right. This will have to do. There's a lot on here that only the Elemental is supposed to know so forgive me the subterfuge. You were probably wondering why I made such a big deal about these tapes in my will. But I knew you well enough, even as a kid that you would honor my wishes and then I just had to hope that luck would play a part, too. It's the best I have for now. Rule number sixteen, don't leave an obvious trail that would give away an Elemental. That's one of those little guys rules."

Bernie snorted, irritated at the mention of little guys.

"Hopefully, by now you've met one or two of them. They can be helpful, especially if the Kashgar have figured out who you are. Beware of them, they're everywhere hidden in plain sight. So, no bank deposit boxes or notes that say, play me. Your preservation is more important than a how-to guide. Each of the tapes is a different lesson for you to learn how to be the one Elemental that will lead them all. I mixed in some of what I've come to believe as well because this job comes with a heavy responsibility. You're going to have to decide how to use this power and for what purpose. It won't be as easy as you think."

The doorbell rang and Bernie hit pause while Maggie went to answer the door and get the food. She came back excited, holding the bags and saw the look on Bernie's face.

"I'm just gonna break it to you quick, Parker. This is a goldmine, no doubt. But a lot of those tapes aren't salvageable. I checked a few already and lots of them have deteriorated. There's nothing left on them."

Maggie felt her heart pounding. "I was so close."

"You may still be close. Come on, if we didn't find these we wouldn't be giving up. We're actually ahead even with just a few clues."

There was a knock at the door, startling Maggie.

"Hello, hey, you ready yet?" It was Diana, already

opening the door. Bernie hit the off button on the remote, turning off the TV and took the bags of food from Maggie.

Diana came bustling into the house in a blue dress with a red floral print and stopped when she saw Bernie standing there, a confused look on her face even as she tried to recover and take it all in.

"Hey, oh, I didn't realize you had company." She looked back and forth between Maggie and Bernie. "Is this...oh hey, are you Jake? Is this Jake?"

"No!" Both Maggie and Bernie shouted at the same moment.

Diana took a step back, hiding a smile tilting her head to the side, just like Maggie. Her red hair was falling around her shoulders. "Okay, got it. Did you change your mind about the Mean Eyed Cat? It's our regular night."

"What?" Maggie pulled out her phone and looked down at the date, spotting a text from Jake. *Have to read that later.* "Right, no, sure."

"Which one is it? Sure or no?" Diana looked at Bernie. "I'm her big sister, Diana, by the way. What you got in the bags?"

"Not Subway, but it is Chinese. I'm a consultant for the police department. A wonk of sorts. What's this Mean Eyed Cat, a pet of yours?"

Diana snickered and came further into the house. "Only the best Johnny Cash tribute bar for miles around. Plus, they serve really good brisket. Has to be better than this Chinese stuff." She took one of the bags from Bernie and opened it, smelling what was inside. "Although this does smell good. What's it gonna be, sister? We can take a pass on one time if you need to keep working." She leaned in toward Maggie and whispered behind her hand, "Although this does violate our rule number four about working too much"

"You have rules!" said Bernie, sounding delighted. "First I'm hearing about it." He pursed his lips, weighing things over. "Johnny Cash bar and brisket? Let's go, I'll put this stuff in the fridge. You need to change." He looked Maggie up and down and said it as more of a statement.

Maggie stared at Bernie hoping there was some unknown magical way to send him a message to cut it out, but he seemed to already be set on going and turned to go to the kitchen, still addressing Diana.

"Who's your friend?" Diana smiled at her sister. "Not like you to make friends so easily and bring them into your territory. I like this new leaf."

"There's no leaf, it's all work related. Just spilled over into here." Maggie shook her head and started for the stairs, heading up to change.

"Go get ready, I'll keep him entertained."

Maggie stopped on the stairs and turned around to say something, but Diana was already out of sight. "No way this cat isn't crawling out of the bag. Oh great, now I'm keeping the conversation going."

CHAPTER TWENTY-FIVE

Maggie came back to the table in the middle room at the Mean Eyed Cat carrying a large plate of brisket nachos. Bernie clapped his hands together yelling in delight, getting a laugh out of Diana.

"You're very enthusiastic."

"This is my kind of food. I love this place!" Bernie looked up at the wall covered in different painted portraits of Johnny Cash, along with a photo of the bar's founder. Underneath was a framed envelope with the original lease written in faded blue ink. On the other wall was an old sign, The Cut-Rite Saw Shop. "What's that? I don't remember any country songs about the mill."

Diana took a sip of her margarita and looked back at the wall. "That's what this place was originally, back when Austin was mostly rural. I think this placed was used for a scene in Chain Saw Massacre, but that was before it became a honky tonk."

"Oooh, movie trivia, even better." Bernie picked up a

corn chip, balancing queso and brisket and opened wide, sliding it in. "Mmmmmmm."

"I want to look away," said Maggie, taking a swig of her beer.

"I'll be right back." Diana got up, headed for the ladies' room.

Maggie saw her chance and leaned in to whisper to Bernie. "I don't think we have this kind of time to be hanging out at a bar."

Bernie sat back in his chair, amazed. "Alright, let's say everything goes south and we don't get the compass back and the earth finally figures out how to get the numbers to add up." He drew a line dramatically across his throat.

"Sensitive, Huldu, go on."

"I don't do sensitive very well and you don't either, kid. If that happens, you really want to remember the last days as a panicked frenzy running all over the place? Or can we mix in some laughs with your family and some really kicking brisket? Honestly, we don't have much more to go on right now. Rule number four." He shook his head even as he pulled out another chip from the platter, weighed down with brisket. "Enjoy being here for just a little while. The earth may have mixed feelings about you, but the universe has your back. Something will pop for us."

"Be here now."

"There you go, and try some of this stuff. Liquid gold, man, you Texans really know how to live."

"What'd I miss?" Diana landed back in her seat, already taking a sip of her margarita. Maggie watched her sister laughing easily with Bernie, someone she didn't know just a little while ago, waving at a regular coming in the door. She took life in so much more easily.

A balding businessman in a suit, his tie loosened came over and held up his beer in the center of the table. "A toast to two of the best from Pressler Street. Man, what a long day."

Diana held up her margarita and Maggie dutifully held up her beer. The man looked at Bernie and shrugged. "Well, come on."

"Hey, okay, didn't know this was a group activity." Bernie held up his beer and clinked glasses.

"I'm Mike, I grew up on Pressler and I've known these ladies their entire lives."

Bernie put out his calloused hand. "I'm Bernie and I, uh, I work with Maggie."

Mike held his arms open wide. "Pleasure. This place is our second home. We used to sneak in here in high school to get a beer or hang out on the patio when life at home was a little too much." He pointed to the bar that was quickly filling up with people greeting each other by name with a hug. "Those are our family, of sorts. That's Deb on the end. I've known her since she got a divorce and worked behind the bar for a stretch. Next to her are Steve and Nicole, nice couple. Hey, Will's already here!" Mike wandered off to the bar, yelling out Will's name.

Bernie looked around, puzzled. "I can't decide if he was trying to tell me to watch myself or welcome me into the fold."

"Knowing Mike, it was some of both. They're pretty protective of Maggie," said Diana.

"They feel the same way about you, and I can take care of myself."

"Never the point, though." Diana gave a crooked smile to her sister. "Just because you can do it yourself doesn't mean you have to."

"Amen to that," said Bernie, lifting his beer. "I like this place. Good vibe."

"This is where we celebrate big events in our lives, me and Diana. We go tubing with all of those guys, play poker, or whatever other idea Mike comes up with."

"There was that guy he found to play gongs when he thought it was important we learn to meditate. That idea didn't really last."

"That's only part of the gang. There are a few more," said Maggie, leaning over to get a better view of the bar. "That's Ralph behind the bar. I think he came with the place and is the reason all of us used to hide out here. You can tell him anything and he'll make you feel like it was the best idea he's ever heard."

Bernie looked over at the slight man with a shock of white hair and an easy smile. He was wiping down the bar listening to someone tell him a story, looking like he was being let in on something great.

"He taught Maggie how to drive. Ralph has even bailed out more than one of us," said Diana. "Not you of course." She gave a nod to Maggie. "Maggie manages to pull off some wild stunts without ever breaking the rules. It's a talent, really. Hey, did she tell you about the time we tried to make our own moon tower?"

"First tell me what's a moon tower," said Bernie.

Maggie ignored them both and pulled out her phone,

glancing down at the text from Jake. He had sent a picture of himself holding up a long receipt and smiling with the caption, 'typical day. Thinking of you.'

She held up her phone and took a selfie with some of the Johnny Cash portraits behind her and sent it, typing, 'out with my sister, regular hang time'. No need to mention Bernie or Huldus or the hunt for a compass. She laid her phone back down in her lap, but it wasn't long before it dinged again. She held it up and saw he had sent a quick note with an emoji of a fox. 'Have a good time with the fam. Love Mean Eyed Cat. Call me when you get home.'

Music started up on the small stage in the other room. Swims with Bears had started playing and Diana had to lean closer to be heard. "Haven't seen you smile like that in quite some time. Text from that Jake?"

"He said to call him later." The smile slipped across her face again.

"I like this," said Diana. "You should try and see the world from a different angle more often."

Maggie lifted her head, surprised as Diana took her hand, squeezing it. "What a good night already. I'm so glad you didn't bow out," said Diana.

"Yeah, me too."

Maggie looked at Diana, who was punching her fist in the air, singing along with the band. "Make your move, no time to lose! Shiver and crawl, we rise and fall!"

Bernie drained the last of his beer and leaned closer to Maggie. "There are a few pixies in here, and one of your buddies is an old elf. Yeah, it's true. That guy Steve is hiding some nice pointed ears under there."

"You think Nicole knows?"

"How do you hide something like that for very long? She has to know." The music picked up and a few people got up to dance. Bernie yelled louder. "We're all stranded in this galaxy together just riding it out on a dirt ship."

"What?" Maggie shook her head, holding her hand up by her ear. "I can't hear you."

"I said we're all stranded in this galaxy..."

Maggie was still shaking her head, straining to hear.

Bernie wound himself up, using his Huldu volume and just as the music came to an abrupt halt, he bellowed, "These are people riding a dirt ship circling the sun!"

The entire bar turned and looked at Bernie and a hush fell over the place.

The singer of the band, Joe Perry grinned and howled into the microphone. Diana laughed as a ripple of howls went through the honky tonk. Mike came over and high-fived Bernie asking, "Can I get you a beer?"

"Ah, a Peabrain's love note. Sure, I'll take another."

"You're our kind of weird, you know that?" Mike walked back to the bar, holding up two fingers.

"I couldn't have said it better myself," said Diana. "I think another margarita is in order."

Maggie watched her sister walk toward the bar, getting greeted all over again by the regulars like they couldn't see her sitting just a few yards away.

Best kind of family. I need to find that damn compass. I'm not done yet.

CHAPTER TWENTY-SIX

The El Camino pulled up in front of Diana's house on Pressler Street, just a few doors down from Maggie's place. Maggie left the car idling and waited for her sister to get out. "Are you sure you don't want me to help you up the stairs. Those margaritas are kicking in pretty hard for you."

Diana leaned her head back against the headrest and smiled at her younger sister. "Since when have three margaritas knocked me down for the count? I'm fine and you know it. If this is your way of saying you need to talk, my door is always unlocked. Or at least you know where the key is hidden. Thank goodness that old guy who broke into your garage didn't figure out we leave keys everywhere."

Bernie slid forward on the back seat. "Old guy?"

"Yeah, some old, short dude broke into Maggie's garage a couple of days ago. Took something of Poppy's, I think." She opened her car door and swung her legs out. "Whew, maybe I am getting a little old for tequila. Can that happen?" She got out of the car and leaned back in, smiling. "Don't forget to make that phone call." She gave Maggie a big wink and for good measure gave one to Bernie. He winked back accompanied by a short laugh.

"What was that about?"

Maggie glared at Diana, trying to get her attention, but Diana was already on to a different topic, happily enjoying her buzz. "Hey, word to the wise. I was at Mom's earlier and they were baking up a storm. Something about Mercury in retrograde and needing something to get over the hump. I hear it was good old-fashioned brownies. She went old school."

"Fair enough, I've been warned."

Diana shut the door and saluted from the sidewalk, turning to amble up her front walk. Maggie waited till she saw her go inside and the lights went on in a few of the rooms.

"What's wrong with a homemade brownie?"

"Nothing, unless Toni Parker made it. Mom likes to enhance her baked goods with something to make you forget Mercury is in retrograde or Aries is floating over Virgo or men are from Mars. Here's another of our rules. Call it a Parker rule number two and a half. Don't eat anything Mom has been anywhere near unless you have an afternoon to devote to doing nothing but eating Doritos."

Bernie shrugged, considering it. "I love Doritos."

Maggie pulled away from the curb, ignoring him and barely hit the gas, gliding down the street till she was in front of her house, pulling into the driveway. She got out of the car, her body aching all over from the past couple of days, barely listening to Bernie talking about how to fix an

M-34 engine that powers part of the Amazon to keep it nice and moist all the time.

A loud *boom* erupted from the backyard followed by a chorus of loud cackling and the chickens squawking.

"I didn't realize chickens could get to be so loud. Do they party when you're not at home?" Bernie wandered up the driveway, curious to see more.

"Wrong on both counts. That's not my chickens." Maggie took off at a sprint for the gate on the side of the house. She stopped halfway there with Bernie right behind her. They both tilted their heads back in time to watch large, translucent bubbles float high in the air, a dark-feathered chicken floating inside each one of them.

"Rhode Island Reds. Those are not my chickens." Maggie watched, hypnotized by the floating chickens until one of the bubbles popped and the chicken flapped its wings in mid-air, not catching flight and plummeted back to the ground, dropping below their line of sight. A loud chorus of deep-throated cackles erupted again. The spell was broken, and Maggie started running again, throwing open the gate and charging inside.

Twenty Huldu gnomes were standing in a circle taking turns blowing bubbles, turning themselves into chickens and floating into the air.

Bernie caught up with her, standing there with his mouth wide open. "This is interesting."

The circle of gnomes spotted Bernie and a cheer went up. "Bernie!"

Bernie smiled and waved. "Hey fellas, what's with the party? I don't remember an invitation."

Maggie elbowed him hard in the ribs, getting an 'oof'.

She watched, eyes wide as another gnome turned himself into a three-toed sloth and attempted to juggle some of his friends, very slowly. Her chickens were running up and down in their yard, flapping their wings in distress. "I will not be getting eggs out of them anytime soon. Did you do this?"

"Kind of, but not really."

"Again with the riddles."

"I put out a call for help after lunch. You got me all fired up to bring out the cavalry, but this..." He pointed at the gnome circus that was taking place in Maggie's backyard. "This is not my doing. I was very specific that we needed serious help and not entertainment."

Two gnomes faced each other, grinning, their eyes half shut as they blew bubbles at each other till they were completely covered. The bubbles glowed pink, sliding off to reveal oversized pink rabbits.

Bernie slapped the back of his neck, trying not to smile, glancing over at Maggie. "Oh, that's a good one," he said. "Wrong time of year, but still, very impressive."

Bernie let out a snicker that built into a laugh and finally, he was bent over bellowing with laughter.

Maggie looked at him frustrated. She smelled the air. "Is it something you're breathing in? Is this a gnome fever?"

A gnome popped back into his usual state and made a beeline for the back steps. Maggie followed him, determined to stop him from going in the house.

"For the love of..." she shouted. There on the back steps was an almost empty plate of brownies. She recognized the pale blue Fiesta ware plate immediately. Her mother had left the plate sitting on the back porch. The note was still propped up nearby.

Maggie took the brownie and the plate from the gnome, pulling it out of his reach when he tried again. "No, no more brownies."

"You sound like you're talking to a four-year-old. Oh geez, hang on, I have to catch my breath." Bernie was still leaning over, his hands on his knees, wheezing with laughter.

Maggie shook her head, trying not to let a familiar resentment creep over her. The only one paying attention to what needed to get done. "Worst imitation of Barnum and Bailey I've ever seen. Thousand-year-old hippies. How long is this going to last?"

"Leo, enough with the Manilow already." The chorus of Copacabana could be heard among the treetops. Bernie stood up straight and wiped his face. "Not long, gnomes have amazing constitutions. Give it an hour and they'll start to come down again. They'll probably pull a few more stunts before that happens. How about we just sit on the back steps right here under the moonlight and enjoy the show."

He patted the seat next to him. "Come on, when are you going to get the chance to see Huldus turn themselves into small farm animals that float ever again? I bet we can yell out suggestions and they'd do it. Huh? Yeah?"

Maggie took in a deep breath and let it out slowly, still holding the plate. *Look at the world from a different angle.* She sat down next to Bernie, resting the plate in her lap and watched the Huldus build a gnome pyramid, taking turns tumbling off the top.

"Do that glowing bird formation you did for Jack's anniversary! Where is Jack, anyway? He's missing all the fun." Bernie peered through the darkness trying to spot his friend.

Some of the gnomes immediately began forming bubbles in their hands, swirling their arms overhead in a continuous circle, raining the bubbles down on their heads. They quickly turned into large, iridescent blackbirds, glowing in the dark and took to the air, flying in a V formation.

"Grackles! Are grackles really gnomes?" Maggie jostled the plate, leaning forward.

"No," laughed Bernie. "Grackles are grackles, well, and messengers." He waved his hand. "Never mind, forget I mentioned that. Story for another day. Oh look, they're making the Olympic rings. Now, that is nice. Go ahead, you call out something."

Maggie thought about it, trying to come up with something. "I can't think of anything."

"Come on, there must be one thing. Think of it more like a magic trick. Hurry up, this stuff is going to wear off at some point and then they'll be all business. I'm the fun one of the bunch, if that gives you any clues."

"Float in the air! I want to float in the air!" Maggie blurted it out. It was the first thing that came to her.

"No, I meant that they could do. Okay, never mind, this should be good."

The Huldus smiled, scrambling toward Maggie and taking the plate from her, one or two trying to get the last of the brownies but Bernie snatched the plate away and held it in his lap. "Maybe that's enough for tonight. Your Mercury is doing just fine."

They put Maggie into the center of their circle and began blowing dark blue bubbles out of their mouths. Inside of each one were different constellations. The gnomes stretched out their arms to the side, and beat the air, faster and faster till it was difficult to see their arms at all. The bubbles floated toward Maggie, surrounding her at first, pushing at her feet and lifting her up into the sky.

She could still hear Bernie's voice below as she floated up to the roof line. When she looked down, she could see that she was floating on top of bubbles that made it look like the night sky filled with stars was just below her.

Her entire body relaxed, bobbing along and she lay back, rolling over so she could look down into the magical night sky. Slowly the bubbles brought her back to the ground and as her feet touched, began to gently pop one at a time. She watched each one, marveling at the sight.

But there in a corner of the artificial night sky was a bubble with a familiar arrangement of four stars in what looked like a random pattern.

'Pop!'

It was gone before she could say anything. She shook her head. "Look at the world from a completely new view," she said, "and tomorrow we figure this out... together."

A Huldu wandered over, weaving a little as he got to Maggie. "You have any Doritos?"

CHAPTER TWENTY-SEVEN

The morning was dragging on for Simon without any relief. He sat behind his desk in the forensics lab and squeezed the compass in his hand, raising it over his head. He was tempted to throw it against the floor, but that would prove nothing and maybe cost him everything.

"Raaaaarggghhhh!" He let out the frustrated scream, shaking the compass and was even disappointed when he noticed that shaking it didn't move the five needles. Nothing was working. He had dreamed of holding this compass from the first moment he read about it. Pictured what it would be like, and when it was finally in his hands, he had rejoiced for days.

Reality was an entirely different experience.

He rested his arms on the spectrometer and put his head down. "Think, think."

"You okay?"

He stood up and whipped around, the compass still in his hand as the color drained from his face. A young detective he didn't recognize was standing in the doorway.

No one ever came to his lab. Most people called first, trying to manage his prickly personality that he carefully cultivated. He glared at the young detective whose eyes widened in surprise at the chilly reception.

"I knocked, you didn't hear me. I was checking on that analysis for the drugs we found yesterday. You okay?" He pointed at Simon's hand. "That's a nice pocket watch. Looks really old. Your dad give that to you?"

Simon ignored the questions. "Your report is not ready yet. Good science takes time." He slid the compass into his lab coat pocket and picked up a flyer off his desk, waving it at the detective. "Here, take this. It's a general outline of how things go on down here. It'll save you a trip next time."

The detective wrinkled his forehead but came and took the flyer out of Simon's hand anyway. "Yeah, sure, didn't mean to bother you. If I could get that sometime today that would be helpful."

Simon didn't answer him, instead he watched him give up and walk back toward the door. "Nothing? Okay." The detective shook his head, muttering, "They did not exaggerate about you, buddy."

"Please shut the door on your way out." Simon waited a moment before rubbing his face with his hands. He pulled out the old diary and opened it again to the place he had bookmarked. "There's only one solution. I have to bring her to me and convince Maggie Parker to help me. Surely, one Peabrain to another she will understand. She will do the right thing. I have to arrange a meeting."

He gently closed the old diary and scooped it up, standing up from his desk and grabbing his satchel. There was no time to waste.

Simon would convince Maggie to stand with her own kind, stand with the Peabrains and use the compass to further the cause and send the Earth back to where it all began. "Send us home," he muttered.

───────

Simon barreled into the squad room, his lab coat flapping open, the satchel slung across his shoulder. "Where's Detective Parker? I need to speak with her."

Moss looked up from his computer, startled for a moment at the sight of the forensics specialist out of his natural habitat. "Uh, Parker and Taylor aren't in right now. They're out on a case. Is there something I can help you with? You know, you could use the phone and just call Parker." Moss said it slowly like Simon was a deer who could be startled at any moment by sudden movement.

"Did they say when they expected to return?" Simon stood by Maggie's desk, looking in every direction like he still expected her to suddenly appear. Moss looked around with him, half expecting to see something himself.

"No, they generally don't. You can never tell how long it'll take on an interview. Try calling her." Moss picked up the desk phone and started to dial.

Simon gave a sharp rebuke. "No!" He caught himself when he saw the look of surprise and annoyance on Moss' face as he put the receiver back down in its cradle. Several other detectives around them smiled, waiting to see what would happen next.

That only made things worse.

Simon wasn't used to kidding around with anyone and

he didn't know how to take it. His eyes flashed darker for a moment, making Moss stand up slowly and walk closer to get a better look. "What the…"

"I mean, I'd prefer to talk to her in person. It's more of a personal nature," said Simon, looking down at his brown Florsheim's before making himself look Moss in the eye. He felt the flashes when they occurred and knew he was losing small bits of time, but he couldn't explain what was happening to him. *Too much stress, probably.*

Moss knit his eyebrows together and looked over at Gonzales sitting nearby. "A personal nature, you don't say? Well, you want to leave a note? Is email out of the question?"

Simon bristled, unsure if Moss was trying to be helpful or was making him the butt of a joke. He slipped his hand into his pocket and felt the metal of the compass. "Never mind, I'll catch up with her later." He turned on his heel and walked out, not wanting to get any more questions. Behind him he could hear someone muttering, "I think that's the first time I've seen him in here."

"No, he comes up about once a year," said Moss. "I guess this means a few more weeks of winter."

Simon felt a rush of anger go through him. He was trying to save them all from a fate they didn't even see coming. "Ungrateful, every last one of them." He shook it off. "I don't have to be liked in order to be right. I'll find a way to get Maggie Parker to listen to me and then, I'll be the hero." His pupils filled in again, turning dark and his fingertips went numb, but the moment passed as quickly as it came, leaving him with a single clear thought.

"Maybe it's time to try a little dark magic again. Nothing else has worked." He headed back to the quiet of his lab, his excitement returning. Surely willingness and good intentions would make up for so many other things. "I need to take this to the next level. No going back."

CHAPTER TWENTY-EIGHT

Maggie got back into the blue El Camino with Taylor right behind her. The shoe store on Lamar Avenue was missing the night's receipts along with a dozen pairs of fly Union LA Air Jordan sneakers. Taylor glanced in the back seat at Bernie licking his fingers after eating a Whataburger taquito with cheese and extra sauce.

"If magic is real, how come you can't just make food appear with your bubbly thing?"

"It never tastes quite right. Kind of like the gluten free option. You want to like it, you know you should like it but..." Bernie stuck out his tongue. "Oh, hey missed a little."

Taylor shook his head, shutting one eye and wincing as Bernie licked the front of his yellow sweater. "Is that thing clean?"

"It's cleaner now." Bernie took another swipe at it with his tongue. "See, there, got out that last bit. Hey, it's Tuesday, I washed my hands."

Maggie pulled out into traffic, heading for the highway, grateful the traffic was still light.

Taylor looked at Maggie. "What does he mean, it's Tuesday?"

"Don't ask. You'll have to live with the knowledge forever if you do. Did you notice that store manager was more upset about those Air Jordan's? I wonder how much those things go for. It's gotta be a couple hundred bucks, easy."

"Thinking of adding to your collection?"

Maggie looked down at her white Veja sneakers with a red stripe. They were one of her few indulgences. "I'm good, but it means whoever stole their money knows enough about shoes to know what to take. They took enough to sell, not to just wear."

"You have that look in your eye. You thinking of where we might be able to find the sneakers?"

"There are a few shady open-air markets around here that sell merchandise for prices that make me wonder what truck the merchandise fell from."

"This is fascinating stuff, really is guys, and I appreciate that you're conscious of the taxpayer's dollar, but can we get back to the bigger picture?" Bernie was leaning between the seats, his arms resting on the backs.

"What is he talking about, Parker? What are you talking about, what is it, Ernie?"

"Funny, making up the wrong name for me. It's Bernie, Mr. Detective. Didn't your partner tell you anything about our quest?"

"Not now, Bernie." Maggie kept her eye on the road,

while still reaching back, planting her hand firmly in the center of Bernie's chest and pushing him into the back seat.

Taylor let out a snort, popping a piece of gum into his mouth.

"I'll take one of those." Bernie's large hand came over the seat, hanging right by Taylor's head till he put a piece of gum in Bernie's palm.

"Thank you. Mmmm, peppermint. Like I was saying… Don't bother interrupting Peabrain, I'm gonna keep talking either way. We need allies to get this one done, and he already knows about magic. Rule two is out the window with him."

Maggie pressed her lips together trying to think of a reasonable excuse that could get Bernie to stop talking. Nothing was coming to mind.

"Yeah, we're on a quest." Bernie rested back in his seat. "We have to find a compass, a particular special compass that kind of helps keep the world running smoothly."

Maggie looked in the rear-view mirror and saw Bernie give her a wink. She rolled her eyes wondering what was coming next.

"Is he for real? Doesn't the Earth just take care of itself?" Taylor shook his head, looking back at Bernie. "That's a big leap to go from you being a mouse to an entire world run on a compass."

"Not exactly what I said, but I can see where there are a few key pieces missing. Tell him it's important, Maggie Parker." Bernie's voice became more serious and he slid forward again, hanging on to the back of her seat. "Tell him the truth or I will. You know I'll rule number four him, mostly because despite our original meeting I actually kind of like you and we need some help right about now."

Maggie dodged around a minivan of kids, their faces pressed against the window making faces at her. It made her think of Diana and leaving her behind. "What about your Huldu brethren eating me out of all the junk food I could find at HEB, even as we speak?"

Taylor threw up his hands, a questioning look on his face. "I don't understand what's going on and I don't tend to like that situation."

Maggie knew she'd gone as far as she could trying to solve this with just Bernie. She was glad she had the excuse of looking at the road while she asked for help. "Here's the short version because I don't even grasp the long one yet. You know that bodega robbery I got caught in the other day? Bernie stopped a bullet that was meant for me." She could feel Taylor glaring at her and could hear him sputtering, searching for just the right swear words to yell. He was so mad, nothing but broken syllables were making it out.

"I should have told you, but in my defense, you weren't in on the magic thing yet and telling you I got pulled away at the last second and put back a few inches to the right wouldn't have been a great explanation. Not if I wanted to be taken seriously."

"There's more I take it."

"Oh yeah, brother is there."

"Not helping, Bernie."

Bernie held up his hands like he even knew how to be quiet for very long.

"Apparently, right now I'm one extra on the planet..."

"Living on borrowed time we call it," said Bernie. "Sorry, zipping it." He pinched his fingers together, running them in front of his closed mouth.

Maggie looked in the rear-view mirror, not feeling good about his odds. "I'll bet you a dollar he doesn't even make it past Manchaca before he's talking again."

"I'm still mad at you but I'll take those odds. What's a dollar? Now spill it, Parker." Taylor rubbed his hand through his white hair.

"I have to jump ahead and tell you about the missing compass." Maggie looked in the rear-view mirror again. "That I caught Bernie trying to steal out of my garage."

"You are the thief!" The veins were standing out on Taylor's neck. Bernie held up his hands like he wasn't allowed to speak.

"That compass was passed down in my family from one special person to another and my father would have given it to me..." She hesitated but made herself say the words. "But he died before he could." She swallowed hard. "Short version like I promised, the compass was taken when we got jacked at the car museum and I need it back for more than one good reason."

They passed the Manchaca road sign and Bernie opened his mouth and took in a deep breath. "Like distracting the Earth so it doesn't keep trying to kill her."

"No one said not to breathe, Bernie."

"I was trying to make things right with Taylor for scaring him with the whole mouse thing. Got you a dollar," said Bernie, smiling and nodding his head. "You're welcome."

Taylor pointed his thumb over his shoulder. "This is who will be saving your life. You're in some real deep…"

"I've already saved her once! I did get her stuck in that tree but that only lasted a few minutes."

Taylor opened his mouth to say something, but he never got the chance.

Dark red bubbles erupted in the street in front of them as people hit their brakes and others pointed. People out on the street scattered. Maggie stopped the car, trying to make sense of it and caught sight of Bernie. He actually looked afraid.

She felt a shiver go down her spine and felt herself calm down, taking a deep breath and looking around more closely, assessing the given information. A figure emerged out of the center of the bubbles, his eyes a solid black underneath a shock of silver hair. "Simon Wesley?"

Taylor pressed the button on his seat belt, his hand already on his gun. "Help, I've fallen into a Marvel comic and I can't get out. I take it Simon is our arch villain."

Bernie had his door open and was creating bubbles in his hand, covering his body till he shrunk down to an over-sized raccoon.

"Tell me that's not your fighting mode," said Maggie.

"We're related to the mighty panda!" Bernie scurried off, sliding under stopped cars till he could take a position flanking Simon under the bumper of a black Ford Expedition.

The deep red bubbles slid off of Simon, sizzling in the roadway, creating a hissing, bubbling pool around his feet that slowly dissipated in steam. He was looking straight at Maggie, a smile on his face.

She got out of the car slowly, keeping the door open between herself and Simon as she pulled out her gun. Taylor got out, gun drawn and came around to the front of the car, calling out to the forensic specialist. "Simon, what's going on here? I've known you for a few years now. This isn't like you. How about we take this someplace quieter?"

Simon looked away from Maggie, the smile dropping from his face. He opened his hands, small red and black bubbles oozing out of his palms.

Taylor pointed his gun, warning Simon. "Drop your weapon of choice, Simon. Come on, you're one of us. We can talk about this."

Maggie clenched her teeth, even as she ran around the front of the car, putting herself between Taylor and the dark bubbles. She had already seen what bubbles could do to human skin. "Back down, Simon. I don't know why you're here, but this will not end well for anyone if you keep going down this path."

Simon held the bubbles in his hands, not doing anything with them, yet. He tried to smile again as if he wanted to reassure Maggie. "I needed to get your attention."

"I'd say you have it, but it can't be so you could put on this show. Tell me what you wanted to say, but can we do it at the station? I can give you as much time as you need."

"That part of my life is over," he said, shaking his head as his silver bangs slid across his face, framing his dark eyes.

Maggie looked at him, studying his face. She had never had much interaction with him, but something was off, making him unpredictable and more dangerous. *His eyes are usually blue.* The back of her neck tingled, and a cold chill went through her. "Why does it have to be over?" She held her ground, her stance wide. She lifted her chin and smelled the air. There was the faint scent of lavender and rotten eggs. *Dark magic, great.*

"Parker, what are you doing?" Taylor had come up right beside her.

She didn't take her eyes off Simon. "I'd tell you to get back, but I know you too well. Can you somehow circle around behind him?" she whispered to Taylor, relieved when she saw him move back unnoticed.

Simon seemed to only want her. *Good, let's keep the mayhem to a minimum.*

"Why does it have to be over, Simon?" She held his gaze, waiting for an answer.

He held up his arms in frustration, pleading his case. His moment to tell his story had finally come. "The veil between one reality and the other is getting torn away. It's only a matter of time before others learn the truth. I have to make sure they hear the *real* story this time." The bubbles melted from his hands, disappearing and he beat his chest with his fist. "We have forgotten who we really are and where we belong. This is not our planet, not where we were supposed to stay."

He reached into the satchel, still hanging off his shoulder and pulled out the leather diary. "I have proof! We are warriors from another place and time meant to live far away from here. It's our birthright, but if we're not careful, we could end up on the wrong end of a deal. There are things you don't know Maggie Parker, but it's not too late. You can fix everything. You are the Elemental I've been searching for." Simon slipped the compass out of his pocket and held it up so Maggie could see it.

Her eyes widened in surprise and she could feel her heart beating faster in her chest. "Simon, you have the compass."

"Yes, yes I do!" He was delighted at his reveal. "And I can show you how to use it. It's all in this diary." He held it over his head. "Together, we can ensure..."

A man drew too close to the red slime still in the street and called out in pain as the bottom of his shoes melted. Simon roared with anger at the interruption, losing himself in the dark spell taking over his mind. He raised his arm, black shiny bubbles appearing in his hand, aiming at the man lying on the ground, even as others went to help him.

Taylor emerged behind the crowd, pushing his way through and raised his gun, firing off a shot, the crimson slime rising back up to swallow the bullet, protecting Simon. The air stank with the mixture of lavender and rotten eggs.

His rage only grew as he spun around, throwing the bubbles into the crowd, scalding a woman as she ran. She fell to the ground, rolling over as Taylor holstered his gun and picked her up over his shoulder to get her to safety. Maggie was preparing herself to take a run at Simon, clearing her mind to think about nothing and set an intention at the same time. She clenched and unclenched her hands, knowing she had to do it. "At least I go down fighting."

She started running, just as a streak of gray and black striped fur flew past her, leaping over the edge of the slime, digging its sharp raccoon teeth into Simon's thigh, biting down hard.

Simon gave a guttural cry of pain, wounding Bernie with a series of bubbles but the raccoon held on, growling and biting down harder, even as he grew weaker.

Finally, Simon was able to pull him away, throwing him into the air, limp and bleeding. Maggie ran underneath, catching the heavy raccoon against her chest, even as the dark red bubbles grew frothy, consuming Simon once again and he disappeared from view. Simon was yelling out in frustration, the diary still gripped in his hand. "Maggie Parker, no!"

A spark ran through her body, ending in a shock at the back of her neck, her eyes flashing with light for just a moment. A hum went down her spine, leaving her feeling nauseous, but she swallowed hard. *Worry about what that means, later.*

Huldus appeared on every corner, circling the crowd and blowing clear translucent bubbles that caught their attention, mesmerizing them, absorbing the memories of the last fifteen minutes and floating away with them. A stout Huldu with a shock of brown hair held up a bubble to blow at Taylor. He raised his gun in response and said, "Think again. I'm already in on it." The gnome shrugged and pivoted, catching a woman in a suit and pearls, her face still in shock, and her mouth hanging open. The bubble splashed over her as her face gently relaxed and she looked at the gnome, puzzled and smiled.

Another gnome bent down over the wounded man, blowing pale purple bubbles over his body, alleviating the burns and restoring the shoes.

Maggie laid Bernie on the ground, still in his raccoon form. His breathing was shallow, and his eyes were shut. "Bernie! Bernie, say something. I'm not sure what to do for you. Take you to a vet, or an ER." She took off her jacket, wrapping him in it against the cold.

Jack came running over to them, kneeling down beside his friend. "Oh, Bernie, that was something. I saw the leap just as we got above ground. It was amazing, brother."

"Can you help him?" Maggie rubbed the gray fur on the top of Bernie's head.

"Of course." Jack waved to two other Huldus. "Brothers, lend a hand." The Huldus gathered, hovering their hands, palms down just over Bernie's furry little body. Bernie stirred but didn't open his eyes as pale purple bubbles rolled across his body. The air was filled with the scent of strawberries. Bernie's body began to shiver and shake, and Maggie tried to push her way back beside Bernie to get them to stop but the Huldus gently pushed her back. The fur receded and the limbs lengthened and in no time, there lay Bernie, a gnome once more.

Jack looked up at Maggie. "That's the best we can do for now. He took direct hits at close range. He'll be fine but it'll take a little time. We'll carry him back with us."

"I want to talk to him first."

Jack saw how determined she was, her hands firmly placed on her hips. He moved aside, gently nudging his fellow gnomes. "Let her in, she's not your average Peabrain. It'll be okay," he said, nodding reassuringly. They all looked at Maggie, waiting to see what she was going to do to their friend.

Maggie knelt down beside Bernie, his eyes still closed

and took his hand. "Bernie, thank you. That was one of the bravest and weirdest things I've ever seen."

Bernie opened one eye and looked at her. "Sometimes what's needed is one good raccoon bite."

Maggie let out a laugh as her eyes filled with tears. "I thought you were a goner and I was going to have to finish this quest alone."

Bernie opened both his eyes and tried to lift his head but the other Huldus pushed him back. "Leave me alone, fellas, I have something to say and I'm going to say it."

"Stubborn till the end," said Jack. "Go on, Bernie, take your victory lap."

"You're not alone, kid," he said, squeezing Maggie's hand. "You're a Peabrain and you're not even using the best part about being a Peabrain. Oh geez, you don't even know what that is, do you?" Even the other gnomes were rolling their eyes at her.

"What, what am I missing? It's that hidden magical peabrain, right?"

"Maggie, no, it's your ability to rise above anything and when it seems impossible, suddenly cooperate for a common goal, even when it benefits someone else. Even when it means the end of *you*. I saw you about to make a run through those bubbles." He poked Maggie with a thick finger. "It's your humanity, it's even named after all of you, for pete's sake. Don't run away from your basic chemistry, use it."

"I can't do this without you, Bernie. Whatever Simon's become, it looks pretty nasty."

"What? Who said I'm not coming right back? This is gonna take a night, tops."

"He's a Huldu after all, not a Kashgar," said the gnome behind his head.

"Those tall bastards," said Bernie, smiling at Maggie. "This is our quest and now we know who has the compass. Big leap forward."

Maggie's phone buzzed in her pocket and she slid it out, reading Jake's text. She felt the tightness in her chest ease.

"It's her new boyfriend," said Bernie to the crowd of Huldus. A general 'ooooh' went up from the group.

"He's working late at the CVS," muttered Maggie, reading aloud, as she put away her phone. "He always manages to text just after a near death experience. Weird. I'll answer him later. What?" She looked up to find every Huldu was staring at her, including Bernie but no one would say anything.

"It's rule number four, isn't it? You already don't like him. Okay, I get it. It's like I have a hundred uncles all of a sudden."

"When's that next date?" Bernie tried to push himself up on his elbows.

"You're not going, so you don't need to know."

"I'm going, it's final."

"I'm grown, you're not going. This is outside the quest scope. My mother can't go, frankly she can't meet him for a while. That's way too risky. She'll ask him his sign, when he was born and tell him we were siblings in a past life. That will be a hard thing to forget. No, you're definitely not going either."

All the gnomes looked at each other, not saying a word.

Finally, Jack broke the silence. "We need to get Bernie home. We'll have him back, good as new tomorrow. Come on, a bunch of little men all hanging out in the street together is an Instagram picture for sure. We need to break it up and get moving."

They helped Bernie off the ground, walking away till they could get out of sight to an area of dirt and grass and disappear beneath the ground. Maggie called after them before they got too far away. "You're not going, Bernie, that's final!"

Bernie lifted his hand to wave, looking back at her, not saying a word.

"Damn that rule number four. What are you not saying?"

CHAPTER TWENTY-NINE

Maggie stood in her bedroom, her hands on her hips. The moonlight was pouring in her window, casting a shadow against the yellow chenille bedspread.

"You can do this." She saw how helpless she was against magic and didn't like the feeling. *That has to change. Parker's don't avoid.*

She breathed in and shook her hands by her sides. "Empty your mind and make an intention. Okay, I want to make a damn bubble." She squeezed her eyes shut and held her hands out. "Bubble, bubble, bubble." Her eyes popped open, with just a little bit of hope that something had stirred but she knew better. "Nothing."

She looked out the window at the backyard and the moonlight against the grass. Gertie was still up, pacing the wire fencing. "Maybe a change of scenery. I can go commune with the tree and Gertie."

Maggie grabbed her jacket and ran downstairs, past the old metal-topped kitchen table that had belonged to her Pops, out the back door and down the few steps. She took off her shoes and felt the cold ground beneath her feet. "Have to love an Austin winter." She knelt down beside the fencing, putting her fingers through to stroke Gertie's feathers, soothing the chicken. "There, there Gertie. All the pretend chickens have flown the coop. You have the place all to yourself now."

Gertie scratched at the ground and looked at Maggie. "I should get a dog, Gertie. I'm not sure petting a chicken is giving me the full girl's best friend experience." Gertie flapped her wings, ruffling her feathers before heading for the short ramp into the coop. Maggie stood up and brushed off her pants, looking around the yard.

"Okay, enough Parker. Time to make the bubbles." She clapped her hands together. "I can do this, yeah, said that. Where to start?" She approached the one large tree in the backyard and stood in front of it, her hand tentatively out, inches from the bark. Her other hand was turned palm up. She pressed her hand against the tree and gasped with pleasure as once again the hum ran through her and she could hear the network of trees sharing information.

Melting snow in Muncie. Need to share the runoff.

Cankers on the leaves of a stand of oaks in Richmond. Too much stale air. Need the wind to move on through.

Exposed roots on cherry blossom trees in Washington, in need of cover.

A cool thread of energy ran through her head and the back of her neck tingled as her mind became clear. *Set an intention.* "How about you show me?"

The ground rumbled and Maggie pressed her hand harder, keeping her eyes closed determined to make a bubble. Make some magic. "Wait, wha…" She felt herself falling, a whoosh of air rushing past her, and when her eyes sprang open there was only an inky darkness that made it impossible to see anything. She paddled her feet, trying to find something solid and stretched out her arms, but there was nothing.

She hit solid ground with a thud, jarring her knees and the light grew around her from the ground up, revealing a chamber and tunnels and copper-colored pipes running along the walls. Underneath was a swirl of blue tile, pointing out into the tunnel. "I'm underground! I did it! Not a bubble exactly, but okay. You showed me something, alright." Her heart was pounding, and she was breathing hard as the realization hit her. "How do I get back out of here? Hello?"

She took a step, testing the ground, still not sure there wasn't another layer to fall through to an even deeper level. "They could stand to put in an elevator." The ground held and she walked further, glancing down the different tunnels, picking one. "That is literally a light at the end of a tunnel." Her voice echoed off the walls and she had to duck down to fit inside the tunnel. She came out the other side, into a much larger area with a mosaic on the floor made out of hundreds of small colored tiles, swirling in different patterns. "Follow the pattern. We're not in Kansas anymore." She went down another tunnel and saw two Huldus chatting, about to turn the corner and head straight for her. She ducked into a narrow side room and found herself faced with hundreds and hundreds of vials, all labeled carefully with the name of an herb, a flower, a root or a leaf. *Chamomile, Echinacea, Feverfew, Milk Thistle.*

She took down Anise Hysop and lifted the glass top, breathing in the smell of licorice. "What is this place?"

"It's our apothecary."

Maggie jumped almost knocking over a row of bottles, holding her hands out till they stopped rattling. She turned to find a gnome with a shock of silver hair peering through the glass bottles on another row of open shelves. "I recognize you," he said. "You're the Elemental. Bernie and Jack have been talking about you." He came around the shelves and put out his hand. "I'm Radar, you're Maggie, right? You made quite an impression on Bernie and he doesn't take to Peabrains easily. Actually, he doesn't take to anyone very easily. Is he with you?" Radar came around as Maggie backed toward the doorway.

"I left him in the cafeteria," she said, lying. *Rule number four will have to suck it.* "I got lost down here, which way is that?" She wasn't ready to find help just yet and get out of there.

Radar smiled and walked up beside her, already poking his head out to the right and pointing down the tunnel. "That's easy to do down here if you aren't a mechanic. Follow the tile along the floor and stick to the navy-blue pattern. Each color represents a different system. That blue is food supply. It'll lead you to where we grow things or the vending machines. Hey, that was a Bernie idea!"

"What's the red tile for?"

"That one is for the engine room and to find the system of the main pipes that keeps things moving for the old ship." Radar patted the wall. "You know these things weren't meant to run forever without being serviced. Little tough out here but it's amazing what the crew has been able to do. Thank goodness we packed for everything before we left! That oil reserve was a lifesaver more than once. The green is for private quarters and the orange is…" He cleared his throat. "Top secret. Has to do with Huldu magic, we don't really share that one. We have to be careful just how much we share with Peabrains, you understand, right? It's never gone exactly the way we hoped. We've made it a policy to let Peabrains progress with magic at the pace they can handle. Rule number thirty-three. We can only guide." He smiled nervously at Maggie like he had said too much. She smiled back at him thinking the same.

Maggie heard Huldus coming from the opposite direction and slid out of the room, still waving at Radar as she followed the blue tiles, winding down different tunnels. She came to a crossroads and looked down at the tile, turning toward the orange and looking back over her shoulder. The coast was clear.

She hurried along, touching the wall for balance as she kept her head down, ducking under the perpetually low ceilings. She was determined to see if there was something that could help her take a shortcut and learn magic.

Her hand brushed a pipe, cold to the touch leaving a blue glowing residue on her fingers that she wiped on the wall. It clung to her skin, still glowing as she picked up the pace, searching for an opening to a room or another tunnel.

CHAPTER THIRTY

A general broadcast went out, echoing down the tunnel, the message hanging in the air. "Keep an eye out for the lost Elemental, last seen looking for the cafeteria." It was Radar's voice with a nervous tremor. "Help her get topside *immediately*."

"I think they're on to you, Parker." Maggie heard the approach of footsteps and took off at a run, ducking down just in time underneath a large metal pipe. She came to a set of stairs carved into the Earth and leapt down, sliding on the gravel, and losing her balance.

"Oof," the wind was knocked out of her and she rolled a few feet, dropping down into a room tucked behind a wall. She lay on the ground for a moment, gathering her wits, getting up and brushing off her pants. The orange dirt clung to her everywhere and her hip was sore where she had landed. She lifted her hand to get her hair out of her eyes and lights nearby came on, illuminating first at the floor and gradually working their way up the walls. She moved her arms up and down in large circles and even more lights came on, further lighting the entire room.

Maggie tilted her head back, relieved she was finally in a room where she could stand up straight. The ceiling soared a hundred feet over head and the room stretched out as far as she could see. The entire thing was filled with shelves that stretched toward the top.

The orange tile ran right along the floor, in and out of the shelves. She moved quickly up and down the shelves, looking at the tall ledgers and pulled down one, opening the large book and leaning it on a shelf. Inside was a list of names, a line of numbers under a column marked 'date' and an inventory of items under a column marked 'luggage'. "The original passenger manifest," she whispered, quickly turning pages. She closed the ledger and carefully maneuvered it back on the shelf, running her hand down each spin, marveling at them. "This is a hall of records."

The broadcast went out again, bellowing down the hall, Radar sounding even more anxious. She knew her time was running out. She ran down one aisle until she got to a break and turned left, running over two aisles and turned right again.

There were books of every shape and size, all hand sewn. She scanned the titles looking for anything useful that she might be able to take with her and spotted a small book in the 'E' section entitled, *Basic Elemental Spells, edition MCC*. She opened the book and was relieved to see it was in English.

"I think she went this way." Two gnomes were in the vast room with her, searching for her. She could hear a beeping sound and looked down to see that the blue gunk still on her fingers was keeping time. "It's a tracking device! I've been tagged." Maggie slid the book under her shirt, tucking it in to the front of her pants and zipping up her jacket. She wove her way around the different aisles, listening to the beeping pick up and eventually came face to face with the two Huldus, their eyes widening as they looked at Maggie, looked at the room she was in, and looked back at Maggie.

"Hi fellahs," she said, smiling, doing her best to catch them off guard and put them at ease. She quickly decided to take a lesson from Bernie and just talk to distract them. "I hear you're looking for me? I got a little lost. It's really amazing in this place. Have you been through this room? I still haven't found the cafeteria. What kind of things do gnomes eat? I mean Bernie seems to be willing to eat anything as long as the ingredient list is super long and starts with sugar or palm oil."

The two gnomes looked at each other again, a look of surprise still planted on their face. Finally, the slightly taller Huldu blinked, gathering his wits and held up a finger. "Wait right here, I'll be right back. Don't take your eyes off of her."

Maggie smiled at the remaining gnome, turning away from him but not moving off the spot where she was standing. She took in a deep breath and let it out slowly. *Clear your mind and set an intention.* The cool thread of energy returned to her head and she felt the back of her neck tingle. "I can do this," she whispered, feeling a rush of energy. "Put me back above ground. I want to..."

She felt the same sudden rush and a zip of wind, the rest of her sentence getting swallowed in the darkness.

"Hey!" yelled the gnome, but Maggie was already gone, headed for topside in the blink of an eye.

***

She pulled her arms in, not sure about the reentry and found herself standing on an unlit trail of the Barton Creek Greenbelt. She recognized the trails from all her days of running and took off in the direction of home. "Next time, I include an address in that intention." She looked under her shirt to make sure the book was still intact and was secure and kept running. The blue slime on her fingers was still glowing and felt warm to the touch. She stopped long enough to try and rub it off on the grass, but it didn't work, and the heat only intensified till it was uncomfortable. She tucked her hand in her jacket and kept going, anxious to get home and look at the book. She ran for a mile, easily covering the ground and even enjoying the chance to be along the Green Belt at night under the stars.

Up ahead, she saw flickering lights and slowed down, her instincts as a detective taking over. She realized as she got closer that someone had set fire to the path just ahead, cutting off her way home. She turned to go back and heard someone call her name as the blue glow intensified on her fingers till it felt like they were burning. She blew on her fingers, but nothing changed and looked over her shoulder, realizing the fires were getting closer.

"There she is, grab her!" At the front of the pack was Simon Wesley and standing next to him was Frank Winters, surrounded by four other followers of Simon who were all holding lit torches above their heads.

Maggie had no time to think and reached inside of her jacket for her phone, but it was gone. "Damn, must have fallen out in Huldu land." Her gun was securely locked away at home. She shook her head, pressing her lips together, willing herself to calm down. *You want to win this one, Maggie, you're going to need to think. No wait, stop thinking. That's what Bernie meant. Feel your way through.*

She let go of analyzing what was in front of her and held her arms out to the side, setting a clear intention. *Kick their ass and take that compass back.* The rest she left up to the stream of magic to find its way. *Don't tell the magic how to do it, what has to be done.* A determined smile crossed her face.

Frank Winters sent out a similar stream of bubbles that had almost strangled Maggie before, this time armored in a shiny metallic coating. They hovered just within feet of Maggie pushing against something but unable to go any further. It was working, she was holding them off. *Don't think, let go.*

Simon stopped a few yards from where Maggie stood, a hand on her hip, the other held out in front of her. She recognized the green puffy coat he was wearing and the stream of magic rolling through her head stumbled for a moment. A few of the bubbles pushed forward, throwing Maggie back, her head hitting the ground. She shut her eyes in pain for a moment, but quickly recovered, scrambling back to her feet and setting the same intention, and letting go. She heard her father's voice echo in her head, momentarily remembering what he sounded like. "You can do this, Maggie." The bubbles continued to push her backward as Simon and his followers advanced, but she stayed upright and let out a breath, the cold stream crawling through her head. *Kick their ass and take that compass back.* It was her only thought.

A new string of opaque bubbles flew through the air, aimed at her legs but they passed a certain point and fused together, raining down on the ground into a milky fluid, absorbed by the ground. Maggie raised her hands, feeling the cold extend down her arms as bubbles emerged in her palms, glowing brightly. She remembered her days on the softball team and lobbed them at one of the torchbearers, easily knocking him out, extinguishing his torch.

Simon looked surprised, and then impressed, a small smile coming across his face. She lobbed the second set of bubbles, taking out two more followers, putting out their torches. The path was becoming darker and harder to see. Simon crossed his arms over his chest and muttered words under his breath, too low for Maggie to hear.

He slowly opened his arms as a stream of pulsing blue light swirled in front of him, slowly taking shape as a rope covered in blue thorns. Maggie's cheek twitched, but she remembered what happened when she lost focus. *Let it go, trust in this source. You are the Elemental.*

The rope slithered around, circling Maggie, unable to get close enough to whip around her. "Kick their ass and take that compass back," she whispered, not giving any further instructions. "I am the Elemental." The rope hesitated, swirling in the middle as Simon worked feverishly, uttering the words over and over again trying to get the spell to work.

Maggie could feel a pressure building in her head and a pain along the back of her neck, but she refused to stop.

She held out her hands again, stretched toward Simon and watched as the rope hesitated and then turned, whipping back at him, curling around his leg and yanking, hard. He fell to the ground, startling Frank who froze where he was, unsure what to do next.

"The compass," whispered Maggie, as the rope curled inside his pocket and deftly picked it out, flinging it through the air to Maggie. It landed in her hand and began to make a whirring noise, the needles spinning as the tiny cogs behind it spun, faster and faster. The round knob on the top of the compass popped open, pushing it up at an angle and small, metallic wings spread out to the sides, fluttering as the compass once again took flight. "I finally have it back." She felt a strong hum pass up her arm and down her back, into her legs, rattling her teeth.

The needles spun around, faster and faster as one of them settled on Maggie.

Simon pushed himself up on one elbow staring at the compass flying just above Maggie's hand, his mouth hanging open. Frank Winter went to toss another string of armored bubbles at Maggie, but Simon put out his hand, "No, wait! Let the needles spin."

Maggie locked eyes with him and realized the secret she was about to let out in the world, lifting her hand and grabbing the compass, not letting it complete the rotation of the needles. Simon looked pained and let his hand drop. "Now, do it!"

Frank unleashed more of the armored bubbles, pelting Maggie's line of defense. She was growing weaker, unused to having to focus for so long and let the magic work through her. Eventually several of them made their way through and one hit her square in the chest, knocking her to the ground. The compass rolled out of her hand and Simon easily scooped it up.

Behind them, the sound of sirens grew closer as firetrucks arrived at the Greenbelt. Maggie saw her chance and whipped her leg around, knocking Frank off his feet and stopping the barrage. Simon turned and ran, already blowing bubbles, immersing himself in them.

Maggie took off at a run, straight for him but she was too late, passing through the air where he had once stood. She kept on running, deeper into the Greenbelt and cutting back when she was safely around the firetrucks, slowing down as she headed for home. She had held the compass for just a little while, again and realized something. The compass had started to speak. It knew where the other Elementals were hiding, if only she could hold it long enough to find out. "Soon enough."

CHAPTER THIRTY-ONE

She ran until she reached her mother's house and went up the stairs, stopping to grab the key from under the middle pot filled with a cactus. She went down the main hall and out to the back porch to the spot she knew to find her mother. She would be there till the early hours of the morning.

"Mom, what's the weather been like?"

It was her perpetual opening query at this time of night with her mother. The answer would tell her if a conversation was possible tonight or her mother was already too far along in toasting the moon.

"It's so pleasant out here. Come sit next to me. The wind has died down and you can hear the coyotes."

There was still time. Maggie went and sat next to her mother on the Adirondack recliner. Oscar slept on the ground by their feet. Toni looked over at her daughter and took in the remaining blue glow on her fingers and the bruises on her arms. "You've been into something. Can I pour you a glass? It's just wine, no fun additives."

"Sure, I could use a glass. It's been an interesting week."

Toni poured a glass and handed it over to Maggie, taking another longer assessment. She picked up her glass and drained what remained in the bottom. "How much do you know?"

Maggie leaned her head on her mother's shoulder. She was used to this roundabout way of getting to what mattered. Conversations that mattered always took a little time and patience with her mother. "I have no idea." She pulled the book out from under her shirt as her mother's eyes widened in amazement.

Toni poured herself another glass of chardonnay and held her hand out for the book, even while taking a large sip from her glass. "Where did you get this? Does anyone know it's missing yet?"

"I stole it, kind of right out from under them."

Toni smiled, holding up her hand for a high five. "You get that from me. Your father would have been more upfront and asked for it and let it go when they told him no. Not wrong, just different."

That perception was one of her mother's better qualities. "So, you know plenty."

"I know I'm an Elemental."

"I believe there's a distinction with a difference," said her mother. "You are *the* Elemental. I took a look through your garage. Someone took the compass?"

Maggie slid her arm under her mother's, pulling herself closer. "A couple of different types have had their hands on the compass. I even held it twice and watched it fly." She fluttered a few of her fingers that were holding onto the wine stem. "It holds secrets."

"So I've been told. Do others realize yet just who you are? Oh look, there's a wild turkey creeping down the alley. Can you see it? Only in Austin."

"Way too many, Mom. It's becoming a little dicey for me."

Toni turned her head and stared into her daughter's face. "Then I guess it's finally time." Toni drained the rest of her glass and got up from the chair, wobbling a little as she made her way inside. Maggie followed close behind her as Toni made a beeline for the living room and pulled a key out from a hidden spot under the mantle.

"I never knew that was there."

Toni looked back at Maggie. "That was the point. You and Diana are relentlessly curious. Telling you no would have only increased your determination to discover. It's one of the best qualities the two of you have. It's delicious that you share it together." She smiled and held the key up in the air. "This goes over here." She walked to the old writing desk positioned in a corner of the room. It had been passed down for generations and stood as more of an art piece than anything else.

Toni crouched behind it, wobbling again but she stayed upright and pushed with her thumbs on the back to the far right with a gentle pressure till a piece popped out, revealing a keyhole. She slid in the key and turned, making a drawer drop down below and stop halfway, positioned between two small ledges on either side, holding it in place. "This was all your Dad's idea. The man loved a good puzzle and could work a band saw. He made the modifications to this old desk. He said no one was ever very interested in it, it was too small, and it wasn't of much value. Made it the perfect kind of safe. Overlooked."

Maggie drew closer and looked at the short leather and brass spyglass resting in the box. Toni pulled it out and slowly extended it to its full eighteen inches. "The Parkers have a few tricks up their sleeves too." She held it out for Maggie. "One of the last things your father told me was to make sure and give this to you when the time was right. He said I would know, and I guess he was right."

Maggie could smell the heavy, sweet odor of wine of her mother's breath. She took the spyglass from her and held it up toward the window, catching the light. She expected to see the street but instead, the telescope was displaying rapidly changing longitudes and latitudes. "What's it doing?"

"It's telling you where every magical is located. It can also tell you what kind of magical they are..." Her mother gave her a sly look, which was always the signal to think beyond what her mother had just said.

The realization washed over her, and she felt a thrill run down her back. "Like an Elemental."

"Clever girl! Come on," said Toni, getting up on her feet. "Let's go back to the porch. There's still a little wine left."

"What about the compass? Does this mean I don't need it?" Maggie trailed behind her, gently carrying the spyglass.

"Oh, you still need it. The compass can do far more and it's necessary for the engine. But back when human beings all still remembered that magic resided in them, they came up with a plan B in case the compass was ever lost. Looks like they knew what they were doing." Toni found her way back to the Adirondack and sat down, already lifting the bottle and pouring a healthy fill for herself and her daughter. "I suppose this is like your graduation or confirmation or something. You are now officially a woman."

"I have been one of those for a while, Mom. The city pays me to carry a gun."

"Well, now the Earth will reward you for carrying a telescope."

Maggie bit her lip, not willing to tell her mother the rest of the story. She was living on borrowed time and with every day, things were getting trickier.

"I'm gonna' head home, I'm worn out." She leaned down and hugged her mother, breathing in the smell of her perfume. "I love you, Mom," she whispered into Toni's hair.

"I love you more," said Toni, kissing the side of Maggie's face. "Come back tomorrow, I'll make some cookies. No funny business, I promise." She drew a small 'x' over her heart.

"I have to work, Mom and you lost your x drawing privileges with Diana's last birthday cake."

"That was all in good fun." She batted at the air. "No one was driving and you two were determined to keep it short."

"Well, you got us on that one. I think I slept on your lawn."

Toni let out a laugh. "I still have the pictures! That was a good one." Her words were starting to slur. It was time to go.

"Nice, Mom." Maggie gave her a crooked smile.

"I'm sorry your father isn't here to present you with that," said Toni.

"I know, Mom, me too." Toni was slipping into the old

memories and would pull them out one by one, sometimes till the light started to break in the sky. Maggie didn't like staring at the past with her anymore. It was too much. "I gotta go, Mom. I'll stop by tomorrow." She cradled the book and the spyglass and turned to go.

"Really nice weather for this time of year," said Toni, taking a sip.

"It really is, Mom," said Maggie, as she walked down the hallway and out the front door, shutting it gently behind her.

CHAPTER THIRTY-TWO

M aggie woke up to the sound of someone clapping near her head. "Wake up, wake up! You are wasting precious time!"

She lifted her head off her pillow just enough to make sure she was still in her own bed. It seemed pertinent given the events of the past week. She half-expected to find out she was outside under the old tree. No, still her bedroom.

"Bernie, personal space! Get out of my bedroom." She looked toward the window and saw the it was still dark outside. "What time is it, anyway?"

"I don't know, must we argue about time? I'm feeling better!"

Maggie opened her eyes again and looked at Bernie turning around in a circle with his arms out. "See? Good as new, maybe better. I've been cutting back on the bacon lately, I think it shows."

"I may have missed you briefly." Maggie put her head back down on the pillow and shut her eyes. "Go away and come back when it's light outside, and most important of all, Bernie, the Huldu gnome, wait downstairs."

"Nope, no can do. Time's just rolling by and we haven't found the compass yet."

"Well, technically for about five minutes last night, what, still tonight? It found me."

Bernie sat down hard on the edge of her bed, bouncing up and down, excited. "You had your mitts on it and lost it? Was that before or after you broke into the Hall of Records? That's right, kid I heard all about it." He slid her phone out of his pocket and put it on her nightstand. "You lost something. I got a pass on this one since I was out of commission. They're blaming that gnome, Radar. He fell for the old, where's the cafeteria line."

Maggie gave up and finally sat up, pulling up her covers. She glanced over at the clock by her bed and saw that it was only four in the morning. "Nothing good happens at four in the morning, Bernie. If someone calls you at this hour, you brace yourself. No one sets out to do anything righteous at four in the morning. Those people, the righteous ones are all still asleep."

"Rule followers, every one of them. I should know, I live with a lot of them."

"You're a rule follower." Maggie swung her legs over the side of the bed and headed toward the bathroom. "Follow me in there and I kill you, Bernie."

Bernie stopped halfway. "Right, right, fair enough. And I'm a rule follower of sorts. I bend a few, every now and then as necessary."

"Okay, I'm a rule follower, I'm a robbery detective."

"Yeah, ironic that you stole something from us."

"Borrowed temporarily because literally my life depends on it and you were down for the count." She crossed the hall and shut the door to the bathroom and went to pee. "Quit standing right by the door. I can't pee if I can see your shadow."

Bernie took a few steps back, still talking. "I'm on your side, I think you did the right thing. I forgot all about that book and every little nugget of information helps. Let's get to it, where you have it hidden? I searched downstairs but didn't find it."

Maggie finished washing her hands and dried them on the hand towel hanging nearby. She opened the bathroom door and looked at Bernie. "You searched downstairs? We really have to have the talk. I can see gnomes are not very good at boundaries." She pushed past him and shut the door to her bedroom before he could follow her inside. She found the pants from last night and held them up to see if they had any questionable stains of blood or blue goo on them. "All good, perfect," she said, stepping out of her pajama bottoms and stepping into the pants.

"Possessions aren't really our thing. You know, magic and all. We can pretty much come up with whatever we want anyway." Bernie's face was close to the door and he was whispering loudly.

"Except fast food."

"Yeah, that's a real gap in magic, if you ask me."

Maggie pulled a UT sweatshirt from under the pile of clothes on the chair by her door and was about to smell it when she heard something small ping against her bedroom window. "Does no one text anymore?"

Ping, ping... ping, ping. Small pebbles were hitting her window.

"Alright, alright, I'm coming."

"Good, are you decent yet?" Bernie whispered through the door. Maggie ignored him.

She went to the window, lifting the sash and looked down on her front lawn. There stood Jake with a handful of pebbles and he was just about to throw another one at the window when Maggie poked her head out. A grin broke out across his face, deepening the lines around his eyes.

"Jake? What are you doing here? Is everything okay?"

"Yeah, I tried texting you but didn't get an answer." He looked down, trying to figure out how to start. "I got this weird text, I think it was from your mother. She said I ought to stop by, sooner rather than later. Oh, and bring coffee." He reached down next to him and picked up the two travel mugs. "She had a lot of exclamation points."

Maggie leaned on the window sill, a feeling of happiness swimming in her belly. "How did my mother get your phone number? Never mind," she waved. "It's like some weird super power she has."

Jake laughed and held up the coffee. "She said something about a Mrs. Fletcher who knew Larry at the HEB, and it didn't really make sense after that. Come on down! It was a good idea."

"Be right there."

Maggie grabbed her jacket and pulled it on over her pajama top, slipping into a pair of worn loafers. She checked her hair in the mirror by the door and combed it with her fingers, fluffing it up in the back. "Will have to do." She opened the door and was nose to nose with Bernie, startling them both.

"Are you ready?" Bernie's hot breath hit her in the face, mixed with the faint smell of strawberries.

"I almost kind of forgot you were here."

"How is that even possible? I've been talking the entire time."

"It all washes over me at some point. You have to go, Jake is here, and he brought coffee. If it's black, he may be the one." She pushed past the gnome and headed for the stairs. "You gotta go, at least for the next hour. Make that two." *Hell with the new underwear.*

"No, wait, I can't go anywhere. You don't understand. Jake may not be who he says he is."

Maggie stopped on the stairs and looked back at Bernie. She could see Jake on the front lawn through the glass in the front door from where she stood. "Explain and make it fast."

"I'm not supposed to, and I may be wrong."

"Good enough, I'm going, you're not." Maggie started back down the stairs.

"I have to follow you, I need to make sure you're safe."

"You follow me, and I ditch you on the quest, and you know I can do it. Or at least I'm learning really well how to do it."

Bernie stopped where he was. "Fine, but I'm nearby just in case. We need a safe word. Yell out peaches if you're in trouble."

"Who yells out peaches?" Maggie opened the front door and held her finger up to her lips. "Shhhh."

"That's why it's a great safe word," whispered Bernie.

She pointed at him like it was a warning and slipped through the door, a smile already growing on her face.

He waited till she pulled the door shut and he ran the rest of the way, easing the door open just enough to let himself out after he had blown enough bubbles to change into a mouse.

Maggie walked over to Jake, trying not to break into a jog. He held up one of the travel mugs to her and leaned forward, easily sliding his tongue into her mouth and biting her bottom lip. She had her hand around the mug and leaned in, letting her weight fall against his chest, this time on purpose and stood there on her front yard kissing Jake over and over again.

She finally pulled back and smiled up at him. "This is going well for you. I chose necking with you over coffee. Unheard of before in my timeline."

Jake smiled and leaned down, kissing her again.

Hell with it, coffee can wait. I can make more.

She finally pulled back again, still leaning against him, his arms around her back. She put her hands on his chest, still holding the mug.

"Your mother seems nice in her texts," he said, laughing.

"She's not like your average mother, encouraging someone she's heard me talk about to come over in the middle of the night and bring hot beverages."

"You talk about me to your mother. That has to be more good news."

Jake slid his hand under her jacket and pajama top and

she felt a shiver from his cold hand against her skin. "Sorry about that," he said laughing.

Bernie ran to the edge of the porch and sniffed the air, his whiskers twitching. He let out a squeak, scampering down the stairs and ran closer, covering his eyes with his paw.

"You want to come in?" asked Maggie, taking Jake by the hand.

"No, not that," whispered Bernie. He sniffed the air, trying to detect a Kashgar.

Maggie pulled him by the hand toward the house, passing by Bernie.

The mouse panicked and Bernie blew tiny bubbles into his hand, blowing them into the wind behind Maggie. They popped one right after the other, releasing a string of fart noises followed by a sizzle and a faint smell.

The expression on Maggie's face froze and she spun around, still holding onto Jake's hand, her face reddening in the dark. She scanned the ground looking for Bernie and finally spotted him. He raised his little mouse front paws and shrugged, running past her toward the house. She swung her foot out trying to stomp on him but missed and watched him squeeze through the opening in the door. He was back inside the house changing into who knew what.

Jake was smiling, his chin tucked down. "That's no big deal. Means you're comfortable with me."

Maggie smiled, pressing her lips together. "I didn't... I mean, it wasn't..." She let out a resigned sigh. "Sorry about that. Too much dairy." She did her best to laugh and was relieved when he pulled her close again. "Can we just sit on the front steps? Maybe it would be nice to bring you inside with a little more planning."

Jake let his shoulders drop and sighed, but he was still smiling. "Of course, this was only meant to be a coffee run, anyway. It was about to be the world's best coffee run..." He laughed and sat down, pulling her into his lap. "It still is."

She wrapped her arm around his neck, setting the travel mug down on the steps, completely forgetting about the coffee and making out with her boyfriend till the sun rose over the trees.

CHAPTER THIRTY-THREE

Maggie yawned, walking through the house, touching her fingertips to her lips, still feeling the sensation of Jake's mouth against hers. Bernie was fast asleep on the blue sofa in the living room, snoring softly. Maggie stopped and unfolded a blue afghan, pulling it over him. "I'm going to let it go that you're right by the front window," she whispered.

She tiptoed away, walking through the house and stopped halfway through the kitchen, smiled, lifting the edge of her pajama top and scratching her belly. "Never did try that coffee." She looked out the window. "Sun's up now, might as well stay up."

She went through the motions of making coffee, distracted as she waited for it to brew, holding up the toaster to get a better look at her face. "No beard burn, good work Jake." She went to the cabinet and pulled out her favorite mug with blue flowers on it and leaned against the counter waiting, almost nodding off.

A flash of bright light and the sound like a lit fuse

coming from her backyard jolted her awake. She ran for the back door, ready for anything and hoping the chickens were alright.

There in her backyard stood a man who looked more like a bald-faced grizzly bear dressed in a heavy tunic, chain mail covering his arms and long pants with leather boots that came up well past his oversized knees. Maggie turned back to run upstairs and get her gun but saw that he was already halfway to the door. She opened the pantry and leaned in, grabbing the metal baseball bat she kept there for protection and ran out the door to get in the first swing. Surprise might be her only weapon.

"Bernie!" she yelled out. "Peaches! Peaches!" But he was still snoring in the other room, moving his feet in his sleep like he was running.

Maggie lifted the bat to her shoulder, leaping off the back steps and got ready to swing, giving it everything she had in her. The chickens were all out of their coop and were flapping their wings, flying up for a few inches and coming back down again.

The beast of a man put out his hand and stopped the bat in mid-swing, lifting it up higher, dragging Maggie off her feet with it. She swung around, kicking as hard as she could in every tender spot she could reach, finally making contact.

The giant dropped the bat, doubling over as Maggie landed on her side, rolling over to get to her feet and try swinging again.

"Wait, wait." A booming voice came out of the man as he held up his hand. "Is this always the way you greet visitors to your house?"

"This week it is, especially if you show up in my back-yard at sunrise unannounced."

He gripped the bat around the barrel. "I can see your point. I come as a friend, an ally really. Did Bernie not mention us?"

Maggie stopped pulling on the bat and relaxed her stance. "You know Bernie? What are you?"

"Give me a minute. That was a pretty good kick."

Maggie leaned the bat against the back porch and went back to the large man, her hands on her hips despite being dwarfed by his size. He finally got his breath back to his satisfaction and spread his arms wide, releasing a spray of dark blue bubbles, covering himself till he turned into a tall, slender man with long straight dark hair.

"The outfit changed sizes with you. That is a cool trick." Maggie held out her hand to help him up and saw that he was still several inches taller than she was. "You don't get to go any further till you tell me who you are and why the dramatic entrance. I saw the flash of light."

"That was my way of knocking on your door." He ran his hand through his hair. "I'm afraid it backfired on me. Let me start over. My name is Wilmark, and you are the Elemental." He pointed to a crest printed on his tunic. "I'm part of a society, thousands of years old that was formed with the sole purpose of protecting the Elementals. We are known as the Knights of Godwin."

Maggie stared at him, rubbing her temple. "What now? One break in to my garage and people are coming at me out of the woodwork."

"You've already been attacked, I apologize. My arrival was delayed."

MARTHA CARR & MICHAEL ANDERLE

"You drink coffee?" Maggie turned to go back up the stairs, grabbing the bat. She didn't even wait for a response. "This will go better if you just say yes."

"Then, yes." He followed her up the steps and into the kitchen.

"Take it black? A secret group of knights are out there protecting the world. I kind of like knowing a bunch of Peabrains have my back."

The knight smirked, clearing his throat. "Not all of us are Peabrains. I'm an elf." He waved his hand over his ear, the light glowing around it for a moment as the ear grew more pointed. He waved it back and the ear rounded again. "It's a simple light spell to make it easier to be among the common people."

Maggie tilted her head, narrowing her gaze. "That outfit doesn't make it tough to blend in?"

"I can tone it down when I have to. This seemed like the right moment to bring out the old outfit. We've been waiting to find one of your kind for a very long time. The records were all destroyed…"

"I heard about that from Bernie and Jack."

"You've met Jack, too. Well then," he got down on one knee and bowed his head.

"Whoa, what are you doing?" Maggie's eyebrows were raised, wrinkling her forehead.

"I pledge my life to you, to protect you and keep you safe till the mission is complete and the engine of the ship is finally put back together. All of us who can rightfully say we are the Knights of Godwin, do the same. We are at your service, no matter what, no matter when."

Maggie pressed her hands to her cheeks. "You can't

hang around me all day, or even part of the day. I'm a detective and there's no way to explain you. I already have a boyfriend, or at least I think he is, so that excuse is out."

"I don't need to be right next to you all the time. We will be nearby, keeping watch."

"Nothing creepy about that at all."

"I can also help you to learn magic. I was a teacher before I was asked to be a knight."

Maggie poured a cup of coffee, slurping it while it was still too hot. "There are still knights in this world. This is one of the weirder things this week." She slurped again. "Trust me, that is saying something, too. Hey, how do I know this is the real you and not that large, hairy guy."

The elf arched an eyebrow at her and tilted his head. "I suppose you'll have to wait and find out. Do you know where the compass is?"

"I do but I'm not sure how to get it back."

"Then that is our first quest. Are you ready? Is that what you're going to wear into battle?"

"You were born in relatively recent times, right? Who talks like that? Hang on, I have to change, this is not my battle wear, and I have to wake up Bernie."

The knight started to say something but Maggie stopped him. "I know what you're going to say. Save the compass, save the world, and buy me more borrowed time."

"Just hurry," said Wilmark, looking out the window.

"You think I'm in real danger." Maggie felt a familiar tingle on the back of her neck and looked past the knight, into the empty backyard. *Find the compass, save the world. I can do this.*

The story doesn't end here. Maggie is on a quest to get the compass back, but will things work out with Jake? Will she be able to find the other Elementals and put it all together in time to save her own life? Continue the adventures with *The Gnome's Magic* now available on Amazon and in Kindle Unlimited.

Join the Facebook Group today and find out about contests and giveaways.

Get sneak peeks, exclusive giveaways, behind the scenes content, and more.
PLUS you'll be notified of special **one day only fan pricing** on new releases.

Sign up today to get free stories, including the prequel to *The Magic Compass.*

CLICK HERE

or visit: https://marthacarr.com/read-free-stories/

The release of this first book in a new world is a kind of celebration for me. The ideas for Terranavis Universe have been percolating in my own brain for a few years now. It's been a test of my mantra, everything happens when it's supposed to... because I dragged my feet for a while.

I have talked about the series, asked others what they thought, wrote a short story to test the crowds, but have never actually gotten around to launching. (And more than one person has had an opinion about the series name – being me I responded by adding it to every title on every book... it's how I roll)

Too many other things to do and elements of this story are very special to me. I wanted to do it justice.

But just about a year ago, I finally quit my day job, which I loved, and tried my hand at publishing on my own – only to learn I don't like it. This is the start of having everything under LMBPN – a team that for me is more like family.

I have also finished moving into the dream house,

unpacked and fixed whatever needed to be fixed. Even planted a lot of azaleas and a couple of trees. I'm out of excuses (for getting out there and dating more too, but that's another story for a different day).

And one more thing that really clinched it. In October of 2018, my very clever big sister, Diana, who I called 'D' died suddenly. D was the one who first taught me about Star Trek, and DC comics and making elaborate costumes and magic and flaming cherries jubilee. She was fun personified mixed with large servings of curiosity. She tackled her fear of heights by taking flying lessons. For the first month of lessons they just taxied, but eventually she flew everywhere in her Cessna.

We were a lot alike and looked a lot alike too. (She was much better at math, however) Time ran out for her way too early, way before the adventures were over.

I stood by her bedside in the hospital and realized it was time for me to start. You see, the fun part of being here is taking on the new challenges, trying that creative thing, risking failure and realizing once again the sense of victory. And to do the whole thing with a crowd of people, the more the merrier.

In other words, it's the experiences that count – not the things. That's what D taught me.

Losing her is what got me to finally quit the day job and sit down and write. The sister in The Adventures of Maggie Parker, Diana is loosely based on D who read my books, still sent a check for my birthday long after I was grown, and an Advent calendar at Christmas, and always had a special way with the Offspring – my son, Louie.

And – bonus - writing the Maggie Parker series will be

a chance to spend some more time with D and the memories and let it sink in – we are all magical, but we have to use it. It's her gift to me to just keep going, reaching out for more to see what the world still has to offer.

The idea that human beings are naturally magical is something I've believed for a long time. Look at what we create, or the way we'll come together and solve a problem, or sometimes say just the right thing to comfort someone in just the right moment. We're amazing! But we can take it all for granted and forget.

So, Maggie Parker is starting to remember and step out of her protective shell. She's even trying dating with Jake. (I may even learn a thing or two about that topic just writing about it.) Too bad that's more complicated than she realizes – and it's unfortunate the Earth wants to self-correct and wipe her off the planet. But maybe the compass can help her solve a few things. We'll see... come on this trip with me – there's a lot more adventures to follow.

Here's my new mantra - Never leave what's most important to the last moments. Do those now. More adventures to follow.

AUTHOR NOTES - MICHAEL ANDERLE

DECEMBER 14, 2019

First, thank you SO much for reading our stories! We can't do what we do without engaged fans.

Today, I want to introduce you to another person "behind the scenes" here at LMBPN Publishing.

You have seen his work on MANY of the books LMBPN has published, including *Witch of the Federation*, *Animus*, *Scions of Magic*, *Judge, Jury and Executioner*, *Magic Ops*, and many MANY others.

I met Jake Caleb at the Boston Fantasy Fest project in May of 2018. He had a booth at the event (as did LMBPN), and I had been looking for a person with a new feel for our covers. I wanted something a bit more raw than photo-bashing, and he happened to have one image from a cover that sealed the deal for me.

It was a crazy female with a white-painted face and marks. It was badass as well as emotional.

I believe our first project might have been *Animus*, but frankly, I don't remember. Since then, Jake has probably done well over fifty covers for us, and if he hasn't, he will soon.

I just went to his website to see if I could find and share the image with you, but he has changed his website (jcaleb-design.com) to mostly show his covers and a submission contact part at the bottom.

I noticed he said he has availability starting June of 2020… So I sent a request to 'purchase' his available slots.

I wonder what he will think about that? Heheheh.

We reached out and asked Jake some questions to give a little better perspective on the enigmatic artist, and here are his answers and perhaps a comment or two from me.

1. **What turns you on? Badass Book Covers**
   (Seriously? Your wife must be pissed.)

2. **What turns you off?**
   Terrible Book Covers

3. **Who do you most admire? Why?**
   My mom for her unwavering good heart

4. **What profession other than your own would you like to attempt?**
   Writer *(I can help make that happen, I know people – Mike.)*

5. **What profession would you not like to do?**
   Teacher *(I thought I wanted to be a teacher at one time. I was provided the chance to teach two people Visual Basic for Applications. I had NO desire to teach again after that week was up.)*

6. If heaven exists, what would you like to hear God say when you arrive at the pearly gates?

Bruh, next time, read the instructions. (*BWAHahaha-hahahaha.*)

7. What is your favorite movie?

Revolver (What? I don't know this movie. I'll have to go look it up.)

From Wikipedia:

Revolver is a 2005 British-French crime thriller film co-written and directed by Guy Ritchie and starring Jason Statham, Ray Liotta, Vincent Pastore, and André Benjamin. The film centers on a revenge-seeking confidence trickster whose weapon is a universal formula that guarantees victory to its user when applied to any game or confidence trick.

8. Who is your favorite character, and from what book by which author?

Black Thorn, *City of Kings* by Rob J. Hayes (*Great, another item to look up <grin>*)

9. What is something most people do not know about you?

I can hit a target from thirty yards with an axe.

(*Good to know. Stay outside thirty yards and dodge like crazy.*)

10. What do you look forward to most in the new year?

The chance to keep growing my business.

11. **What's your favorite non-LMBPN series you've done? What's your favorite series inside LMBPN?**

Non- LMBPN – *Rylee Adamson* series by Shannon Mayer LMBPN – *Witch of the Federation*

12. **Do you have a web site you'd like to promote?**

Sure, my website is www.jcalebdesign.com

I hope you got a little more background from Jake, and check out his other covers. The man is a true artist.

Ad Aeternitatem,

Michael

Other series in the Terranavis Universe:

The Witches of Pressler Street
The Adventures of Finnegan Dragonbender

**If you enjoyed this series, you may enjoy these series
in the Oriceran Universe:**

THE LEIRA CHRONICLES
I FEAR NO EVIL
REWRITING JUSTICE
SCHOOL OF NECESSARY MAGIC
SCHOOL OF NECESSARY MAGIC: RAINE CAMPBELL
ALISON BROWNSTONE
THE DANIEL CODEX SERIES
FEDERAL AGENTS OF MAGIC
SCIONS OF MAGIC
THE UNBELIEVABLE MR. BROWNSTONE
THE KACY CHRONICLES

CONNECT WITH THE AUTHORS

Martha Carr Social

Website:
http://www.marthacarr.com

Facebook:
https://www.facebook.com/groups/MarthaCarrFans/

https://www.facebook.com/terranavisuniverse/

Michael Anderle Social

Michael Anderle Social
Website:
http://www.lmbpn.com

Email List:
http://lmbpn.com/email/

Facebook
https://www.facebook.com/TheKurtherianGambitBooks/